The Hidden Crown

The Return of Magic: Book 1

K.E. Blair

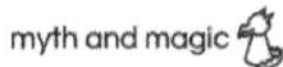

Myth and Magic Publishing

Book Cover by Deranged Doctor Design

Development and Line Editing by Hannah VanVels Ausbury

First edition 2023

For Jessica and Carly, who have spent the last decade hearing about this story.

And yes, I expect you to read it again.

CONTENTS

1

"Girl, hurry along here!"

At the sharp command, Anslee sauntered back over to the chef's side, excuses for her leisurely pace already on her tongue. "Magda," she told the chef, "I was just—"

"I know what you were *just*! Looking at ribbons you do not need, flirting with men you do not need."

Anslee threw back her head and laughed, linking her arm with the older woman's.

"You know we only have enough money to afford meals for our lord and us for the week! There is no extra for extravagancies," Magda continued her chastising.

Market day only came once a week, and Anslee awaited this day eagerly. She wore her best dress of robin egg blue, and her favorite, if old, matching hair ribbon. She was lucky that Magda brought her to the market every Sunday and let her roam around and admire the crowd. Anslee was always scouting, always looking for a potential suitor to entrap. She weaved through the crowd, eying the other junior servants making purchases in the fresh air and keeping her eyes open for eligible young men.

"I guarantee I need all of those colored ribbons and the attention of all of those young men." Anslee winked. "I'll only be young once, as you are always so fond of telling me. Best enjoy it while I can." She flounced off to grab leafy greens to use for the week's meals. After rifling through the choices, she found the least wilted produce and placed a number of coins in the vendor's outstretched hand. She dropped her goods into Magda's outstretched basket. Hopefully, if they were quick to finish their shopping list, Magda would release Anslee, and she could ogle any available young men in peace.

"Hmm, and the change for the vegetables?" Magda murmured, examining the selections. Anslee hid an eye roll before placing the leftover coins into Magda's outstretched palm. She sighed, clasping her hands behind her back.

"What are you doing now?" Magda asked, eyeing Anslee's stance of false humility.

"I'm waiting for my praise," Anslee told her with a straight face. Traffic bobbed around them as they stood still in the street, crushed between stalls.

Magda burst out laughing, ignoring the dirty looks they were receiving. "You're too clever for your own good. But still not worth all those ribbons," Magda said with a smirk.

Little did she know, Anslee needed those ribbons to make a fine first impression. She bit her lip to prevent herself from sticking out her tongue at Magda's backside.

"Come along. Let's at least finish our shopping before you run off on me." The woman continued down the main street of the market, veering off to grab the sundry items on their list.

The sun shone on a tall man with blond hair dressed in velvet and satin at a produce stand two stalls over, and Anslee turned. Could she have spied a target so early in the day? She crept closer, trying to hide behind a group of young women standing nearby a stall of carrots and onions.

One of the girls was showing off a simple, metal chain looped around her neck, as her friends giggled and smiled. "Look! He said this is to remind me of him until he can purchase a proper ring! It's like our promise ring," she said with hearts in her eyes.

Her friends twittered and fawned over her until the old woman manning the stall hacked out a laugh. "Are you three daft? That's an old rumor meant to keep the cows from giving their milk away for free!" The young girls cringed, but the old woman continued laughing. "I can see he didn't pick one too bright either..."

Anslee veered away. She could get her vegetables from someone a little nicer, thank you very much.

She lingered two stalls over, perusing tiny bundles of assorted herbs. Hanging pots dripping live basil, thyme, and dill covered most of the stall, giving her the option of fresh (horridly expensive) herbs or the meager dried bundles. The botanist, a loud, cheery man, leaned over when he saw her linger.

"Anslee, good to see you again!" he boomed. "Stay awhile and chat. The herbs always like you. Why, even the flowers bloom best after you visit." He gestured toward the tall, vivid plants at the back of his stall. Only serious patrons for a great manor could afford those. She never visited inside the stall. She smiled sweetly and stepped away.

"Not today, Robert. You know Magda would never give me enough to afford one of your beauties."

"I bet we could come to an agreement," he rumbled.

Anslee winced. She bet they could, but she didn't want to be involved in that.

"What if I had some information to barter?" he offered.

She fingered the fresh smelling leaves of a basil plant. "Information you think I would be interested in?" she asked, eyes wide. She could be manipulative when it suited her. And information always suited her.

The corner of his mouth turned up in a sly grin, as if he knew the exact sort of information to entice her. "I hear there's to be some big hooley up at the palace." He jerked his thumb north, and Anslee spared a glance, knowing she wouldn't be able to see the spires from this far away with tall, lean buildings crowding the view.

"What's that got to do with me?" she pouted, moving on. The basil leaves had somehow got caught in her front laces, and she removed them, careful not to break the tender stems. Robert didn't seem to notice.

"I know you're on the prowl, young miss. You can't fool me." He winked, and Anslee froze, trying not to blush and trying very hard not to glance at the young blond man she had passed.

"Now I won't tell your good mistress, but you should know that big celebrations mean big flowers. And come with high and mighty visitors crowding the town. You're about to be flush with options, young miss."

Hmm, this was food for thought. Anslee dipped her head.

"Thanks for the intel, Robert. What do I owe you for this? Remember that Magda keeps tight strings on that coin purse of hers."

Robert shrugged, waving her on. "As I said, I just wanted you to have a little quality time with my plants." He looked pointedly at Anslee's hands, which now caressed a baby fern blooming on the corner of the stall. His grin stretched ear to ear, threatening to crack his face in two. "Seems like I got what I needed after all."

Anslee edged away from the stall. Robert was always kind, but sometimes he gave her the creeps. She found Magda at the end of the row, with her mouth full of a half-eaten pastry and sticky fingers. She held back her sigh of disappointment. Taking a break wouldn't take long, but it kept her stuck to Magda's side that much longer. And a fat chance of impressing someone when she was being bossed around by the persnickety chef.

"None for me?" Anslee complained, hands on her hips.

Magda wiped her mouth before passing a few coins to Anslee.

"I'm free?" Anslee asked, her face lighting up in a grin. An entire afternoon on the prowl!

"Consider it a peace offering. Spend it on what you will. But return to the manor in time to prepare supper." Magda shooed her away.

Beaming, Anslee thanked her and ran off toward her favorite market corner. She knew Magda would make her way home for a nice nap and back to the butcher's for her own flirting (not minding the butcher's wife, of course). She, however, was off to fawn over the brightest silks and fabrics she could not afford, and perhaps settle on some ribbons that she could.

The bright sunlight and loud noises assaulted her senses as she escaped from Market Row. She did her best to avoid getting caught in the disputes and gossip that was stirring up.

"Did you hear those dirty roamers are back? Camped out at the edges of the wood again."

"What's this kingdom coming to? I'm sure they're the reason for the increased animal attacks."

She sidestepped around the gossipers and walked until she came to the less trafficked row that contained her favorite dress shop. Magda's guilty pleasure was treats, but Anslee liked something longer lasting. A little daydreaming wouldn't interrupt her plans.

Lost in fantasies of wasting the day away as a rich lady, Anslee's fingers rifled through the most colorful dresses she could find—deep sapphires, twilight violets, and bold garnets. These jewel tones were much too expensive for her, as the shop girl knew, shooting glares across the room. At least Anslee had remembered to keep her fingers clean this time. The only reason the shop girl tolerated her presence at all was because Magda purchased fabric from this shop for the household. Sometimes Anslee was even able to try on some of the more reasonably priced dresses.

Anslee pulled out a pale violet dress with a wide, low collar and a tiny floral design worked around the edge of the bodice, but a stranger grabbed her arm. Thinking it was the proprietor she froze, knowing she could not afford the thing. The dress's skirt swayed at Anslee's yanking, and the clean skirt brushed against Anslee's own dingy skirts. She gripped the dress hanger even tighter before turning to make her case, the lies of choosing dresses for Magda to purchase already rushing to her lips.

Anslee dropped the dress she was holding and fumbled to pick it up, as she gazed up at the most gorgeous man she had ever seen. He had jet-black hair, perfectly slicked around his face, and dark almond eyes. His skin was darker than hers, as if he spent his days constantly outside, but his face and body showed no signs of hard work. His clothes were of the finest material, with dark amber leggings and a coat of chocolate satin with gold thread overlays. Shadows darkened the storeroom, as if the sun had suddenly dipped behind clouds. Anslee wondered if this was perhaps the store owner, coming to revoke her membership of daydreams and perusing once and for all. Her muscles tensed. To flee or not to flee?

"Miss." The man's voice was deep and poured over her like honey. She would have liked him immediately if she had not been gearing up for battle. "This color, really? The fabric is fine, but I must say, the rest of this would just look atrocious on you." His words rumbled over her, speaking to some primal instinct that oozed menace and demanded respect. Anslee froze.

He took the dress from her hands and placed it back on the rack without a care for the wrinkles he left. He stepped towards the more vibrant hues in the back of the shop Anslee had originally fawned over. Maybe he was heading to the back rooms to grab something, like a broom, to chase her out for good. The girl tracked their every move with interest. Anslee debated whether to convince him her mistress would come along with the proper funds momentarily or if she should scuttle out as quickly as possible now. The man's arm darted out, and she jumped, instinctively checking his hands for a weapon.

Instead, he pulled forth a gown from the rack—deep sapphire blue. What was wrong with her? She wasn't used to looking for danger where there was none. She swallowed as he spun to face her, either not noticing or ignoring the way she involuntarily jerked back, as the gauzy fabric of the skirt swirled around their legs. Dark jewels glittered against the neckline. This gown was much more extravagant than the dress Anslee had fawned over.

"Now this would look much more becoming on you, don't you think? A frock fit for a queen." He smiled at her, showing all his pearly white teeth.

This man was beautiful. He was menacing. He was complimenting her? She stepped backward. Shadows seemed to ooze forward, following her. Oh no, she wanted attention, but not this kind of attention.

"I can't afford that dress," she told him flatly. Her pulse was racing. Something about this man set her on edge. She wanted out of this conversation, and out of this shop.

He pulled back the dress, a quizzical wrinkle appearing in his brow. "Have I offended you, miss? My apologies. It was my intent to help you decide on the most becoming dress. I thought this color would show off your best features." He offered a short, formal bow over the gown still clutched in his hands.

He twirled his wrist, and the gown folded itself up and floated over to the counter. Anslee gasped. A mage! She leaned backward, careful to not let any of his magic touch her. The last thing she needed was spare magic dripping on her. Her reaction made sense now. Magic was rare, exceedingly so. She wondered if Robert had been alluding to magic like this, and if more like him would come soon.

"You fear the magic?" he asked, raising his eyebrows at her. He didn't notice the shop girl behind him with wide eyes, slowly edging toward the door. This mage would not receive a warm welcome from the shop owners of Yonderton.

Anslee's neck prickled. She suspected answering him truthfully wouldn't be to her benefit. "The dress is simply gorgeous," she told him neutrally. "Unfortunately," she took another small step back, eyeing the shadows that lingered near his feet, "I do not think I would have anywhere to wear it to."

The stranger's eyes snapped from the dress to her face. His spine straightened, as if he were preparing himself for a formal introduction, and the shadows collected themselves, blinking out of existence. "I do not believe I have properly introduced myself." He took her hand graciously and lifted it to his face to blow a light kiss of air over the back of her palm. "I am Avery Varrock, Lord of the Eastern Whilliswoods, and it is my pleasure to make your acquaintance, Miss...?"

"Anslee. Anslee Yonderton," she repeated meekly. Lady of nothing, she did not add. Like all unwanted children, her surname dogged her wherever she went. She would never be free of the taint of Yonderton. But even if she had a true title, she did not want this man to find her.

"Anslee," he murmured, rolling the name around on his tongue. "Anslee, Anslee. It appears you know nothing of magic."

He seemed surprised by this observation, though she wasn't sure why. He must be new in town to think any of the Yonderton citizens wouldn't be afraid of someone like him. Not when they all knew the history of how magic had left this city drenched in blood. One such as him wouldn't catch us unawares. But she kept her mouth shut, not wanting to anger him.

When it became clear she would not respond, he continued. "Well, thank you for this delightful conversation. I find you most charming."

Anslee blinked. Had they been part of the same conversation?

"I hope to run into you again." He grabbed her arm and kissed the back of her palm before bowing low and exiting the store. Anslee suppressed a shudder until he was out of sight. The folded dress on the countertop lay forgotten. Anslee rubbed her arm vigorously and the hand where he had grabbed her, trying to clean any trace of magic that may have lingered on her skin.

"Of course you brought trouble with you!" The shop girl had made her way to Anslee's corner of the store and was glaring at her. The shop was once again bright and cheery. Anslee stared blankly at her. As if she had purposely brought in a mage with her—the nerve of this girl!

"I've got paying customers coming in soon, and I know you won't be getting anything. Time for you to leave."

Anslee looked down her nose at this girl and held her tongue. Neither of them had been brave enough to confront the magic user, so what if the shop girl used what little social capital she had to kick Anslee out. Some people didn't know how to handle themselves when confronted with power. Anslee thought she had frozen, but she had at least successfully thwarted the mage's attempts to learn about her. The shop girl had drifted into the shadows.

Anslee couldn't blame her for being angry. Mages were dangerous. Who knew what one could do with the right information.

2

Anslee was halfway home when she realized it would be a waste not to spend any of the extra money Magda had passed on to her. That creepy mage had scared her off before she had the chance to purchase any ribbons. She turned around, ready to battle the crowds to the nice vendor's stall she had seen earlier and buy some of her ribbons. Perhaps Magda would even like a nice gray one to match her muddied soul. Magda was nice enough, but why did she have to force Anslee to cut root vegetables for hours every Sunday? Magda acted as a sort of catch-all chef and steward for the manor, and that meant she controlled Anslee's every move. But the vegetables were the worst. Anslee didn't know how anyone could stand to eat as many of them as Magda had forced her to prepare. But when money was tight at the manor, they cooked stew, stew, and more stew. She bustled into the crowded stand, waiting her turn to pick through the colorful fabrics.

Backbreaking work, really, she mused. *Bending over the table, hurting my eyes, chopping those tiny morsels, trying not to cut myself. I should be out picking daisies, making flower wreaths, twirling at balls with handsome strangers.*

She sobered at the thought. What would that handsome stranger... Avery Varrock, he had said his name was. What would it feel like to dance at a ball with him? No doubt, she would wear one of her old dresses, while he would dress in exquisite finery. She harrumphed as she walked along. Would he have still taken an interest in her? Or would he have found her inconsequential, the perfect victim to test his evil magical machinations on? She shivered, whether from her thoughts or the clouds covering the sky. Darkness crept against her vision.

Finally near the front of the queue, she snatched at a handful of ribbons.

And a Lord of the Eastern Whilliswoods? No one even lived out east! What sort of preposterous lie was that supposed to be? How absolutely absurd. Lord of the Whillies, drakes above. Did he even know children called his lands the Whillies? Anslee still remembered the taunts from her own childhood... *Behave, or your parents will throw you in the Whillies and see what gets you!*

They had named it for the forests of Weeping Willow trees that spanned the area. Gorgeous territory, if one was into the monotony and dreariness of that sort of thing. Personally, Anslee could not fathom a single reason she'd ever want to leave the capital and venture east to a place like that. It sounded like it brought only death and sadness.

She forced herself to put aside the dark purples, grays, and blue ribbons she had been holding. She was only thinking about the Whillies and already those morose thoughts were affecting her. No, it would be only cheery ribbons for her and Magda. Some bright pinks, yellows and baby blues. She brushed aside the shopkeeper's offerings of white and tan and settled on the cheery pink hues, and one sage ribbon specifically for Magda.

"Very well, just the one spectrum of the rainbow then?" the shopkeeper asked.

"Yes, one of all the pink ribbons, must I repeat myself?" Anslee asked, annoyed. She shook her head. She had had enough of these shadows that seemed to follow her every thought and make her snippy.

Satisfied with her purchase, Anslee flounced away, leaving the saleswoman happily counting her coins.

Did anyone even live east of the capital's region anymore? She could not think of a single person she had ever met who had lived there. Or even anyone who had wanted to live there! No, the place was simply barbaric. Dirt roads, filthy hovels, a single fortress in a lone town—who wanted to go there? Just a bunch of goats and sheep running around. Probably with a few shepherds to take care of them or such nonsense. A goat herder, perhaps. Some dogs? She shuddered. Her mind flashed back to the conversation she overheard about the roamers squatting outside the capital.

She took out the brightest ribbon she had purchased and wrapped it around her hair. At least she did not live like that. At least she could still enjoy the splendors of society—a few nice ribbons, if perhaps not a nice dress, maybe even a specialty cheese today... That dress cost too much, but she had enough to splurge for that goat cheese that she and Magda liked so much. Drakes above, perhaps she'd even splurge for the footman and the stable boy as well! She enjoyed spreading her minor wealth on the days she had it, unlike some people she had met today, who preferred to just stick it in other's faces. Lord Varrock's face floated through her mind, all clean cut and sharp angles. She harrumphed again and searched her bag for more ribbons. Those would cheer her up.

The best place for baked goods and fancy cheeses was out of the way. She may be later than Magda expected and miss out on the prep for dinner. Hopefully, Magda would not mind once she saw the treat. With her head buried in her bag, she scurried in the opposite way. She turned the corner off Market Row, crashed into another body, and went sprawling across the ground. Someone had whipped around the corner and straight into her! Her bag went flying and her ribbons sprang from her hand, falling in the dirt. Anslee landed on her ankle, giving her a perfect view to watch all of her ribbons being trampled by nearby pedestrians.

"Gosh, I'm so sorry, miss. Here, let me help you up!" A large callused hand gripped her upper arm and hauled her to her feet. She flew upward at his tug, and he caught her before she fell back over. Its owner was presumably the same person who had knocked her over. Anslee pulled her hand free, wiping the dirt and gravel caught in her palms, and using it as an excuse to avoid looking at this inconsiderate person so she would not scold him. Her ribbons peaked out underneath the dirt beneath her and she scrubbed her hands harder, trying to get ahold of her temper.

"And your bag of goods is all over the ground as well! Again, I am terribly sorry, miss. I really wish I had the time to stay and help, but I must be off. Are you sure you're alright?" Those firm hands gripped her arms once more, forcing her to look at him, presumably so he could make sure she hadn't broken her pretty face with her fall. She stared defiantly past his shoulders.

"My god. Anslee?" She looked up at the sound of her name—straight into a pair of familiar green eyes two seconds before he smacked her lips with a loud kiss. She froze.

In a flash, she went back in time to when she was ten years old. Robin's arm wrapped around her, pulling her against him to keep her from running forward to throw herself in harm's way. He punctuated his words with a powerful hug that rattled her more than he probably meant, and she came back to herself with a gasp.

"It's been years! I did not believe I'd ever see you again!" He pulled away, but kept gripping her arm, as if afraid to let her go. As if expecting her to celebrate as much as he was. As if he hadn't just kissed her in the middle of a busy intersection while she was on her way to buy artisanal goat cheese with her pink ribbons lying in the muck.

"Hello, Robin," she said stupidly. "What are you doing here?" She tried to drive genuine warmth in her voice, but warring images flashed in her mind of the last time she had seen him. Or rather, that she had heard him. And the screams. The piercing cries of the horses. A memory she had buried long ago struggled to break free.

Robin threw a brief glance over his shoulder, before turning back and rushing in for another quick hug. She shied away, and he lingered in front of her awkwardly. "I am terribly sorry, but I must be off. It was great to see you! You're still living in the city?" His voice lilted up at the end of his question in a soft accent, one she had purged from her own voice long ago.

Her words caught in her throat, but she nodded.

"I'll find you again then. I've just moved to the area. I hate to leave so soon after finding you again, so I will not say goodbye, Anslee." And he was off, briskly walking away oblivious to the cog of confusion he had thrown into her well-oiled life.

So the rumors were true. The roamers were back in town.

She studied his retreating backside, and couldn't help mentally comparing Robin to his much younger self the last time she had seen him. He had grown from a skinny boy of fourteen into a broad-shouldered man with a brisk, confident walk. His wavy bronze hair brushed the tops of his shoulders, swaying backward with each step. His clothes were a dull brown and hunter green, with well-worn suede boots and accompanying gloves tucked into his belt. Better to fade into the woods and disappear. A far cry from the noble gentleman who had surprised her earlier today.

He turned suddenly, throwing her something from his pocket. She caught it, surprised.

"Something to remember me by!" he shouted, laughing, before getting lost in the crowd.

She opened her hands to reveal a simple silver locket with an acorn engraved on the front. It felt like he had captured her childhood memories and imprinted them upon this silver heart. Any metal was precious to the roamers. For him to give her a trinket made of metal would be a huge financial loss for him.

When she looked up, he was gone.

Just as well, since the constable's men rounded the corner moments later, running at full speed. Anslee stepped out of their way. They would sooner barrel into a lowly servant and complain she ruined their chase than run around her. She fingered the locket, hidden in the folds of her skirt.

Robin was doing well for himself then. He was as charming as ever. And a dangerous threat to the new life she had carved out for herself.

3

The kitchen door slammed open and shut as Anslee rushed through it.

"Hellooo, is that my wayward charge?" Magda shouted from deep within the kitchen. "What goodies have you brought me?"

Anslee considered just rushing through to her room. She was angry, nervous, but mostly tired. She hadn't seen Robin since she was a child, and to add to that her earlier encounter with the handsome mage and the fact she had forgotten to purchase their fancy cheese... She was overwhelmed with no time to process.

"Magda, I am feeling ill suddenly. I need to take the evening to rest," she shouted through the few walls that separated them. "My apologies, but I'll take over the baking tomorrow." She ran through the hall and down the stairs to her room in the far back of the house before Magda could respond. Better to feign sleep than hear a whisper of Magda's disapproval.

True to her word, Anslee immediately went to bed and spent a restless evening tossing and turning. Her sheets tangled between her legs, as she relived moments from her past when Robin and herself would run through the woods.

But dark shadows now followed the two of them in her dreams. They weren't running for enjoyment. They ran in fear, terrified of the unknown that was chasing them.

Anslee woke up, drenched in sweat and clutching the covers, trying to shake the images of her nightmare from her mind. Pictures of law enforcers pooling into their forest campground, demanding justice and killing Robin as he jumped in front of them, trying to stop the swords they wielded from atop their horses. When the ensuing mob rushed forth to attack and demand their justice, Anslee was flung aside, falling to her death before she was suddenly awake. She pressed her palms into her eyes, the dream a crude mockery of what had really transpired all those years ago.

Anslee tried to calm her racing heart, telling herself that she knew Robin was alive. She had just seen him earlier that day. Their run-in must have caused the nightmare. She threw the covers off her body, and cool air rushed over her, prickling her skin in tiny goosebumps. She welcomed the chill though, since it eased the tension from her dream. The cold she felt here and now was real.

In defiance of the fear that had taken hold while she slept, she swung her legs off the bed, wrapping a light robe around her shoulders. A quick walk to the kitchen for a midnight snack would ground her in reality.

She shivered as the cold air nipped at her skin. Leaning against the window, she slowly eased the glass pane down. The town manor had a slight yard out front, with just enough room for a single tree to grow beyond the gate. When she was younger, she had often imagined reaching out and swinging onto the tree's branches to escape back to her freedom, away from the confining rules of the manor and off to run wild in the woods. She was never quite tall enough to reach the closest branch though, and then when she was older, she had no inclination to do so. Where would she go since her parents were gone? And the roamers she had grown up with and thought cared about her were no longer inclined to do so. No, there was no place and no one for her to run to. It was best, her adolescent self had concluded, to stay where she was, where she could at least depend on consistent shelter and meals every night.

She pressed her face against the cold glass, allowing the yellow dappled curtains to cover her body. The gauzy fabric did a terrible job keeping the morning sunlight from streaming in, but they were perfectly fine for a night with a weak moon like tonight. She was ready to turn away when a shadow slid along the wrought-iron gate. She went still. Someone was watching the house behind that tree. Who would prowl around their gates after midnight? She must be imagining the shadowy figure. Her mind flashed back to her dreams. Shadow figures had been chasing her then as well. She didn't remember that happening in her past, but now she was starting to wonder... She shook her head. Impossible. Nothing had been chasing her then, just as nothing was watching her now.

She had waited long enough. No one was there watching her. Determined it was all in her imagination, she lifted her foot to take a step back, and noticed a slight movement, as if a cape had rippled in the wind. It stilled as a hand with long, slender fingers clutched at it, and she saw someone slowly creep away. Should she sound the alarm? Surely they were preparing to break in and steal something from the house. She opened her mouth, ready to yell for help, when the cloaked figure moved *through* the fence. How was that even possible? No, she knew what she saw, and that person—that *thing*—had definitely gone through the fence. Her mind flashed back to the mage she had encountered at the dress shop. She shivered.

And who was she to stop them? But the young butler Georgie was here. And Magda. And the lord. Asleep. A mage wandering the grounds could only mean bad things were afoot. The others had no clue what danger they were in. She couldn't lose another person. She flung her window back open and crawled onto the windowsill before she had thought through her next steps. Her robe pooled beside her, entangling her legs. She had been too scared to jump out of this window as a child, but she was a child no longer. Could she reach the tree branch that had always been just beyond her fingertips? She stood shakily, squeezing her muscles taut to keep her balance. One step forward for leverage, and she jumped. Her arms stretched out... The branch was right there! But her robe caught in her legs, tripping her as she leapt. She stretched but grasped only air.

Anslee hit the ground with a *whoosh*, rolling onto her back and wheezing. So that was what it meant to have the wind knocked out of her. It had been a long time since she had been injured while slipping away for an adventure. She had forgotten how alive it made her feel! And how much it hurt. She closed her eyes for the count of five, gathered her breath, and pushed herself up. After the noise she made climbing and falling out of her bedroom window, she lost any upper hand. She groaned, pulling herself up to her feet. If that intruder had indeed heard her, then she needed to be fast.

Springing towards the gate, she grasped at the bars, looking desperately for the way he had slid through so quickly and quietly. She ran her hands along the top bar, looking for a hinge that would swing open or a missing bar. But the gate hadn't squeaked. She knew she wouldn't find an opening here. She gave up and ran towards the entrance. She had to follow him and see what he was up to. How had he escaped so suddenly? She panted as she pushed through the front, pulling her robes after her as they caught on bushes. Her pulse pounded in her ears. No sign of the intruder here.

She ran around the corner. Shadows chased her. Full stop. Deep breaths. She pressed against the bars, this time on the other side of the fence. No footsteps on the ground. No torn pieces of clothing. Not even any smudged fingerprints to signal a person had been here at all. She placed her head against the bars, sighing deeply. Breathing fresh oxygen back into her lungs. Slowing down her racing heart. What was she doing out here? Racing outside to chase literal shadows. She chastised herself softly. Those dreams had gone to her head. There was no one here.

A low growl erupted behind her. She swung around.

"Who's out there?" Her own unwavering voice surprised her. She had expected a human intruder, not a rabid dog. Her bravado faded as dark shadows coalesced around her. Darkness bloomed upward and outward, unfurling like a dark flower before a midnight black beast swept out. Amber eyes flashed in the glow of street lamps as the beast slunk toward her like a wolf sighting its prey. The shadows cloaked its true size, but she had never seen a dog that large. It looked the size of a bear! The beast's hackles raised as it rumbled a warning. Were those spikes atop its back? Anslee tried to retreat, but her back pressed against the metal bars behind her. Why had she rushed out of her safe house again?

The beast sank into its haunches, preparing to spring. Anslee shut her eyes tight, turning away. "Please, no, please no, please no," she whispered to herself. Her fingers dug in the pockets of her robe for anything that might help her. They came up empty. Daft girl, leaving the house with no weapon. The roamer Anslee would have never. The city had made her soft.

Click. Clack.

The nightmare stalked closer. The beast strode forward on clawed hooves. It bared its teeth at her and growled, ready to rip her apart.

"Help me," she whimpered, praying for someone to hear her. "Goddess, I will happily live the rest of my life as a servant if you help me just this once!" she prayed.

She slunk to the ground, her right hand holding onto the bars to stay balanced. Let the beast think she was giving up. Let it believe she was nothing but a pathetic girl too weak to protect herself. It was close enough that its warm breath lapped over her like ocean waves. She cringed but didn't look away. It padded closer. She reached behind her slowly with her left hand, using her body to hide her movement as she grasped at gravel and small stones. She had one chance to escape. Her hand full of shrapnel, she re-positioned herself, balancing on the balls of her feet. The beast took another step closer, and—NOW!

Anslee sprang forward, throwing her fistful of dirt and stones and whatever she had grabbed straight into the giant beast's eyes. Hearing it howl, but not waiting to see its reaction, she sprinted around the corner and back through the fence. The gate reverberated as it snapped shut with a loud clang, and she slid the linchpin in place, locking it. Why hadn't it locked when she tried to leave?

The door to the manor was too far away. She would never make it. She sprang for the tall oak. No better time than now to learn if she could still scale it! In her childhood, this would have been a breeze. Now her heart pounded, and the blood pulsed through every limb as she scrambled up the side of the tree. She reached the limb that stretched out to her room and paused for a moment to rest, gearing up for the leap she had failed to make last time. The angry growls of the beast rattling the gate shocked her senses. She knew she had little time before the beast tore it down.

Anslee's heart pounded even in her fingertips, pressed against the thin branch with her limbs wrapped around it.

The beast suddenly fell silent. The birds and small hidden things she hadn't realized were still awake also went quiet. Staring at the ground, an eerie, green fog rolled past. The beast whimpered, scrambling backwards and yelping. Anslee swallowed.

There were rumors that magic used to live here. She had grown up hearing them—tall tales meant to keep her scared and hidden in bed at night. Hushed rumors she wasn't supposed to hear about what chased the roamers through the woods. Even as a child she had never paid much attention to them. Magic creatures simply did not exist. She had used to believe that.

But then she met a mage today.

And this night... Her thoughts drifted back to her dream. Was it an omen?

Bone tired, she sat in the tree, waiting for the green fog to dissipate until the sun peeked over the horizon.

She blinked her bleary eyes open. The yard glowed in the bright morning sunlight, and birds chirped, telling each other to wake up and greet the day. She must have fallen into an uneasy sleep. Her bones and joints ached. She slid down the tree, scratching her hands along the rough bark before walking over to the servant's door. A quick survey of the yard showed no signs of the supernatural. She swayed, trying to stay upright. Had it all been a dream? She was so tired.

She stepped inside and snapped the door shut with a definitive click. Whatever that thing had been, it was gone now. And Anslee was beginning to wonder if it had ever really existed in the first place, or if this was her mind playing tricks on her.

4

Since Anslee was already awake, she washed her face and headed downstairs, ready to start the day before the rest of the manor awoke. She felt half dead after being awake most of the night but wouldn't be able to fall back asleep, even if she tried. Magda surprised her when she was halfway through mixing the ingredients for the day's morning bread with her favorite cranberries and raisins (Why not indulge a little if she had to get up earlier to make it?).

"Magda! What are you doing up? I told you I'd take care of things after last night," Anslee said, her hands moving sure and steady as she kneaded the dough. Magda leaned against the door, not making any move to help her.

"I know ya did, girlie. But why should I believe you now? I depended on you last night and you backed out last minute too."

Anslee paused her kneading, realizing that she had truly irritated the older woman. "I'm sorry, Magda. I had an incident yesterday, and it just left me rather startled, is all." She debated telling Magda about her run-in with the mage... but she didn't want to be tainted by the mention of magic.

"Is that why I don't see any of those new ribbons you promised you'd be getting us yesterday, either?" Magda crossed her arms over her chest. Anslee noted she had not put on her apron. At least she knew by the tiny smile that she was just teasing her and not actually angry. A tiny knot uncurled in her chest.

"It had a little something to do with that. I kept one or two of them, though, so I'll bring them down as soon as I've finished this. Did you come down here just to watch me work then?" Anslee teased back.

Magda heated some water over the fire and rifled through the different flavored teas she kept on hand. Their house's owner was a reclusive person, so he seldom had visitors. Staff had free rein of most of the various teas and coffees that would have normally been used to entertain visitors. It was also the reason they had such a lenient head of staff in Magda and household chores. Besides the basic cleaning, cooking, and housework, there just was not enough work left for the rest of them to fill their days (and an absent lord didn't notice idle hands). Anslee was forever taking advantage of this, out living her life pretending as if she were a lady herself half the time.

"No, I'll take my sweet time this morning and enjoy this delicious tea I bought yesterday for all of our visitors."

"Oh, Magda, you know we do not have any of those." She chuckled, weaving the bread dough into plaited rows before placing them in the oven.

Magda laughed with her. "Of course not. But I can appreciate a slow morning while you do all the heavy lifting today." Magda settled into the corner with her tea and produced a book from the folds of her skirts. Magda had come very prepared not to work. She wondered if now was the time to tell Magda about her run-in with magic not once, but twice yesterday. Magda was in touch with all the local gossips. Surely, she would have heard if this had happened before. Anslee opened her mouth, then quickly snapped it shut as Magda settled down into a comfortable chair she kept in the kitchen corner. Anslee couldn't interrupt her respite.

Bread in the oven, she wiped her hands against her skirt, brushing away the flour before she ran upstairs. She had saved at least a few ribbons from their fall in the dirt yesterday and wanted to grab the cleanest before Magda remembered to chastise her again.

A few minutes later, Anslee rushed back into the kitchen. Magda raised her brows at her. "Did you get whatever it was you needed so quickly? I thought for sure you'd wake the rest of the house with your galloping around."

Anslee pulled her arms from behind her back, revealing mauve and sage green ribbons. The coloring offset the icy lightness of Magda's eyes, and the sage one was regal to boot—exactly how Anslee thought of the cook.

"Tada!" Anslee said.

"These are gorgeous, my girl. But they look much finer than the ones you normally bring me. Where are yours?" She darted her all-knowing eyes up to Anslee, who evaded the question. She didn't want to reveal the details of her run-in with a roamer. Gah! That would be even worse than mentioning the mage. At least she didn't have a history of living with mages.

"Tsk tsk. You know I would never buy and tell. Now be a dear and take these before I change my mind." Anslee had felt like being rather generous with her money after that stranger—Lord Avery—had flashed such exquisite wealth before her eyes. He had paraded those expensive dresses in front of her as if their worth was nothing to him. She was jealous of his cavalier attitude towards money and wanted to feel the same sort of power he must experience every day with that wealth. So she had ignored the sensible part of her mind that usually made the purchases, and let the little greedy voice that always wanted more! Nicer! Better! Take control of yesterday's ribbon purchases.

"Thank you, but I think I'll save this one for a more elegant occasion." Magda tucked the green one away before wrapping the mauve one around her head, taming back the hair that had sprung forward in the humid kitchen. Anslee wondered again if now was the time to ask about the shadow monster last night...

"Speaking of elegant occasions, did you hear the news yesterday?" Magda leaned forward, eyes sparkling. Anslee's interest piqued. Thankfully, she didn't have to wait long.

"There is to be a ball!"

Anslee stared. "A what?"

"Are you daft? A ball, girl! A dance! A feast put on by the king and queen of the castle!"

Oh, so this must have been what Robert mentioned yesterday.

"Don't they have those all the time?" Anslee scoffed. "Why would this one interest me? It's not as if we ever attend these things."

"Because, my girl. This time, we *will* be attending."

Anslee laughed. "Are we going out on loan somewhere? Those fancy lords and ladies can't pour their own drinks?" She'd never attended the palace, even as a servant. But if mages were showing up in this city, then what other far-fetched ideas might happen?

"Not at all." Magda's grin split across her face, accentuating her dimpled cheeks. "It's all over the town, my dear! In celebration of, well, not celebration, I suppose. In honor of the anniversary of the missing princess. For the first time, they're opening the palace to everyone who lives in the capital. It's supposed to be a show of strength or something for our enemies and allies. All I really care about is that *we'll* be in attendance!" Her book dropped, forgotten beside her.

Anslee bent down to check the status of her baking bread. "That is absurd. Did you spike any of that tea you've been drinking this morning?"

"I am telling you it's the truth. The butcher told me about it yesterday, and I just had to see for myself. There are proclamation scrolls all over the city. I'm surprised you didn't see them! But then again, apparently, you had a more difficult time than I had expected collecting these ribbons." She fingered the blue one and eyed Anslee out of the corner of her eye. "Perhaps you should go see for yourself."

"Really? But it was my turn to—"

"Go, go already. You've done enough this morning. Go to the main square and read the proclamations. Buy some cheese while you're out. You seem to have forgotten it yesterday. I'm going to finish my book while you're gone." Anslee knew a dismissal when she heard one and flung her apron off and into the corner. She had to see this proclamation for herself. The entire ordeal was unprecedented, and she suspected Magda might pull a prank to get even with making dinner yesterday.

Anslee was exhausted, but she untied her apron strings and left, backtracking her steps from yesterday, making her way through the same path she took every week with Magda. This early in the morning, the streets stood deserted from the normal crowd out shopping. Trees lining the pathway were barely blossoming, and the early morning chill had her wrapping her arms around herself. Had she really fought a shadow beast outside this very house yesterday? It seemed less and less likely as the sunshine suffused the streets and the wind whistled merrily past.

She had forgotten a wrap when she ran out of the house, and she bounced from foot to foot while she skimmed the proclamation she found nailed to the lone lamp post. The parchment curled at the edges, and she had to push the edges of the paper down from the rifling wind. She quickly skimmed the flowery writing.

The 20th King and Queen Dracor of Dracorian Mountains declare a ball in honor of the 20th anniversary of their missing Princess. By order of this proclamation, all nobles, lords and ladies of the main houses are hereby invited. By order of this proclamation, all neighboring nobles, lords and ladies of the Dracorian Mountain territory are hereby invited. By order of this proclamation, all townsfolk of the Yonderton Town surrounding the Dracorian Mountain Palace are hereby invited. We shall hold the ball in honor of the anniversary of the missing Princess on the Eve of Midsummer. Doors open at six in the evening, followed by drinks, dancing and merriment. At midnight, guests shall be escorted out of the palace, and the doors shall close. Through this ball in honor of the missing Princess, may all our people, our neighbors, and our friends recognize our strength through these years. By the Order of their Majesties King August and Queen Clementine Dracor of the Dracorian Mountains, so be this decree.

Hmph, she thought to herself, letting the wind whip the edges of the paper from her hand. A little highbrow for her tastes, but the overall message was good. The ball was in little less than a week! What an excellent opportunity to meet a lord. She'd have to be careful to avoid any mages in attendance, but this could be just the opportunity she was waiting for! A chance to meet someone without giving away her station...

What could she possibly wear to such a thing? Her mood dropped a bit. She certainly didn't have the spare time or money to purchase a dress on such short notice. Another way to separate the riffraff visually from those truly invited. She sighed. Perhaps if she shirked her chores, she'd be able to sew a few baubles onto one of her dresses and give the illusion of riches.

Suddenly, she could not keep the smile from splitting across her face. The Midsummer Eve's ball could not come fast enough!

She ignored the little voice inside her head that whispered this was an excellent occasion for beasts in the night to tear into and devour a crowd.

5

Anslee's steps slowed as she walked back to the manor. The last person she had danced with had been Robin. If that even counted.

She had found a grassy knoll above the roamers' frenzy as they made camp outside a new village, and had been practicing the one ladylike vice that looked enjoyable—dancing. Not the wild dancing they performed after a feast or successful venture into a town, returning with more money than the roamers knew what to do with. The kind where the fire leaped high, and the people danced around it, jumping even higher. Where wild music sang through the wind and through her blood and she could not see the quickening movement around her for the rhythm pulsing beneath her own skin. No, this was the calm, precise movement she had seen roamer women perform with a stranger. A single man had requested just one dance, and as soon as it was determined he only wanted a single waltz and was willing to pay, Lily simply could not refuse. Anslee had seen the greed and cunning sparkle behind her eyes, but the strange man had only seen a beautiful woman willing to give up a few minutes of her time to dance with him. He, Anslee had quickly forgotten, but Lily had epitomized grace, and that was a contradictory image of the callous woman that Anslee could not strike from her memory.

Anslee snorted. If she had met a horrid woman like Lily as an adult, she wouldn't have hesitated to put her in her place. Her vision darkened at her anger, and her shadow leapt behind her.

Anslee found herself beneath a sprawling tree, inedible fruit spoiling on the ground around her as she clumsily practiced choreography she had watched from afar. She did not feel graceful or awe-inspiring. Instead, she felt small and clumsy as she tripped over rotting apples and crumpled to the ground. She kicked the fruit away after another failed attempt. What was the point of learning to dance like this if she had no one to help her? Even Lily couldn't have been so graceful dancing solo. Or maybe she could, *that inner traitorous voice whispered, but Anslee hushed it quickly. She grunted in frustration and walked in a circle before picking up her scraggy brown skirts and starting over with an off-balance curtsy.*

"May I have this dance?"

She jumped a foot in the air at the intrusion and pushed Robin away. Her cheeks furiously blushed rosy. She had thought she was alone. Never would she have pranced around like this if she thought someone was spying on her! She wrapped her arms around herself, hugging her torso and asked if he would run off to tell the others.

Robin pulled back, looking hurt. "Of course not. I'd never do that to you. I came to assist with your... dancing." He grinned at her, and anger boiled under her skin.

"I knew you were spying on me! Leave me alone, Robin, if this is how you're going to be."

He raised his hands up to defend himself from her persistent fists pummeling at him. "Stop that," he laughed. "I came here to help you. I've danced with Lily before, so I know what I am doing."

She paused warily. "You have? Why would you ever want to do such a thing?"

"Eh, my da thought it would be a useful thing to learn. Ya never know when you'll need to woo a woman," he said, pulling at the edge of his tunic collar nervously. He gave a mock bow before offering his hand again. "And now, my lady, after all this persistent chatter, may I have this dance?"

She waited a moment, gauging his sincerity or if he'd trip her or some such thing when she accepted his help. He, likewise, waited patiently until she stepped forward and took his hand. The two of them slowly measured their steps beneath the crabapple tree, Robin concentrating on remembering and Anslee concentrating on Robin. Their dark brown clothes looked like dancing sticks, swaying in the wind beneath the greater forest canopy.

Her shadows wrapped tightly around her, hugging her as she lost herself in the memory. She came to herself suddenly, realizing she had walked right up the steps to the front door of the manor. Robin had been her confidant once upon a time, always there for her whether or not she asked him to be. Shadows fell from her shoulders, crawling away before she noticed them.

She gazed up at the awe-inspiring manor in front of her. Not the largest on the block, but certainly the largest she had ever lived in. She wished more than anything that she could have a house like this. One where she could feel safe and never have to worry about learning to dance well enough to hide the roamer mannerisms she couldn't shake.

6

Well, she thought to herself, *nothing to it but to enter through the front door*. She steeled herself, placing her hand tentatively on the handle and taking a deep breath in and out before flinging the door open. So what if they had never invited her to use this door before? It wouldn't hurt this once.

She waltzed through the front door, surprising Georgie, their butler, who had been dozing against the wall. It was his usual habit since he had no other tasks this early in the day, and no one ever visited this house. He gazed at her with sleepy eyes as Anslee strode past him, acting as if she belonged here.

"Well, I take it ye found the warrant for the ball? Or did you plumb walk right past it? It's been well over an hour since you left." Magda had moved away from her spot in the corner by the fireplace and was onto stirring some mysterious kettle over the kitchen fire. "You should at least believe me now." She eyed her over the edge of her pot. "Do you have the whole invitation memorized or not?"

With a huff, Anslee collapsed in the vacated chair. "It seemed quite pompous if you ask me. And why now, all of a sudden? Why this year? It's not as if anything different has happened to us." She wanted to forget the memory of Robin. He should stay locked in her memories along with the rest of her past. She didn't need to know if he was out there, barely outside the town's borders. Or if he had a family of his own by now...

Magda interrupted her thoughts. "Who's to say why royals act the way they do? They've got different rules than you and I, girl." She picked her spoon out of the kettle, thick lumpy liquid oozing down the sides and splattering as she shook it at her charge. "And who are we to complain about a ball? May as well get our jollies where we can, especially when it's free!" She said this last with an emphatic shake, and chowder plopped on the floor. "Be a dear and clean that up," Magda murmured, hiding her smile behind her hand. Anslee frowned and got down on her knees to wipe up the mess. No doubt that had been on purpose—a subtle reminder that she had not been carrying her weight lately.

Anslee grumbled as she sank to her knees, not saying anything loud enough for Magda to hear and reprimand her, and slid around the floor to catch all the tiny splatters. The soup danced away from her rag. "But is it really a ball that even we can attend? I've never heard of such a thing before."

"Aye, there was once one long ago. The first anniversary of the King and Queen, I believe." Magda stopped stirring to lean against the stove, her eyes glossing over at this faraway memory of hers. Her blue ribbon sparkled, and Anslee could almost imagine her leaning against the castle walls like that, gowned in a fine ensemble of matching gossamer silk. She blinked, and the image was gone, and Magda whispered her memories as if afraid to break the spell. "I was older than you and could scarcely believe my eyes. That was the first time we ever had a ball for us common folk. The king was just so in love with his wife that year that he wanted to proclaim it to the world."

Anslee suppressed an eye roll. More like he wanted to lay his claim, the way any man might, and scare off anyone who wanted his betrothed. Look at me and my big army. Fear us!

"His nobles and court and couriers paid to trail him around like peacock feathers weren't enough, he claimed. He had to show his people—his enemies, his allies, even his old lovers—what he felt for his wife... It was a magical night."

Anslee couldn't stop her snicker this time. She was sure Magda had had a magical night... maybe even with the beloved butcher.

Magda's voice turned practical. "But that was before the famine. One of the last years of providence before he locked himself and his wife up in that castle of his."

Anslee's ears perked up. She rarely heard of a time before the famine. The famine was the reason money was always so tight around the manor.

"What caused them to clam up in the castle?" she asked.

"Enemies stole his babe!" Magda told her, wide-eyed and serious. "Didn't you know? He's been hiding ever since... or looking for her. Too scared to face his people. After that big showy celebration, he couldn't even keep his castle secure." She spun the spoon in the thick stew over the crackling fire. "And now we're the ones who have to suffer for it. I doubt he notices a lack of food on his table. And here we are now," Magda declared briskly. "Wiping the floor and cooking the meals and talking about a new ball about to dawn on us. Not such a joyful occasion as before, but a ball nonetheless."

"Anyhow, some package came for you while you were out. I had Georgie throw it up in your room for you. I've already finished the cooking while you've been out, again, might I add, so you might as well go look."

It wasn't often that Anslee received packages. The truth was, there wasn't anyone to send them to her. Burning with curiosity, she flew out of the kitchen, leaving Magda behind and mumbling to herself in the kitchen about ungrateful serving wenches.

Anslee entered her room to find a much larger package than she had expected, sitting in the middle of her precisely made bed. For someone that grew up in the forests, she certainly kept her space tidy now. Magda had drilled cleanliness into her when she had moved to the city with dirt still under her nails. Roamers sent her there after her chief had claimed to know a couple who had need of a new maid. The gentleman had mostly ignored her, but the woman of the house had really taken a shine to her and spoiled her in place of children that she did not have. The couple did not officially adopt her but coddled and spoiled her as if she had always belonged to them. Once the woman passed away, her husband slowly faded into the background, and Anslee reverted to her status of a lowly housemaid. It had been the closest relationship she had akin to a grandparent, and she had loved the old woman for loving her. But once she had passed, she faded from Anslee's memory, and the house moved on as if she had never existed.

Anslee pounced on her bed, fingering the edges of the box before sliding her nail through the lip's edge and opening it a crack. The box was long and narrow. There was no decorative wrapping or any sign to indicate who may have sent the package, so she hesitated to open it. Who did she know that would send her a package? Her thoughts flashed to Robin, but she brushed those aside instantly. He did not ask where she lived, and she doubted he had the common sense to ask his father where he had taken her all those years ago.

She flung open the box. A single envelope sat atop a frivolous amount of tissue paper. It was a creamy white envelope with her name looped over the front in cursive letters. She had never seen a name so elegantly drawn before. It was a masterpiece of calligraphy and artwork. Tendrils of tiny ivy and flowering buds grew off the "A" in her name, and sliding waterfalls trickled off the looping "l." A soaring hawk swooped off the last swirl of the "e," and the wide range of natural beauty created with simple paper and ink astounded her.

She turned the envelope over and slid out a single card. This one contained a script just as elegant as the envelope's address but without the additional artistic touches. She could tell it was the same hand that had drawn the writing on both papers.

To the lovely stranger I met in the back of Madam's Dressing Gowns, may we not stay strangers for long. I am keen to learn more of this town, and your place within it.

All my best,

Lord Avery Varrock

Her hand dropped to her side. How had he known where she lived? She shivered, and shadows crowded around her. Mages could do unthinkable things if they knew enough about you. She should have protected herself better yesterday. Keeping her hands to herself would have been a good start. So would have walking out as soon as she recognized what he was.

But then again... why look a gift horse in the mouth? If this package contained what she expected, then this dress could be just the item she needed to trick others into believing she was above her station! At a ball, no one would know who she was and dressed like this... it would be easy to mistake her for a lady of renown. It was the perfect stage to capture the heart of a lord.

She gently placed the card to the side and ripped away the delicate tissue paper. No need to let a little insecurity stop her from the delicacy shrouded within this box.

Had he delivered this box himself? Perhaps he simply asked the shop girl, and lord knows, that girl knew Anslee by name, sight, and sound after all the times she had been there! Tissue littering the floor, she gasped as she pulled forth the dark purple gown packed into the box. She tenderly gripped the sleeves to pull it all the way free. The dress unfolded until the luxurious skirts swirled around her. At first thought, she had believed the dress was the same violet gown that she had lusted after at the shop. But upon closer inspection she realized this dress was much more sophisticated. Oh, they were both the same color and had the same stunning details. But the other had a fuller skirt that looked more like a ball gown, a poofy concoction fit for a princess. This dress, however, was made for a woman. The lacelike bodice flowed down the sides of the overskirt and swirled against the gauzy underlayers. When she spun, holding the dress up to her, the several layered underskirts swirled out around her, and she saw equally dark complementary shades fan outward. It was perfect. She needed to wear it and twirl about her room.

Moments later, she had done just that, and the silky bodice and gauzy skirt slid down her body, the skirt pooling softly at her feet. Tiny amethyst and sapphire gems glittered against a neckline much deeper than she had ever worn. The ample amount of cleavage the dress revealed surprised her. It was much more revealing than the modest dresses she wore as a maid, and she blushed even though there was no one here to see it but herself.

Could she push it down a little? Perhaps tuck it back into her dress? No, that certainly did not work. Now she was just moving them around. She sighed and put her hands on her hips. Perhaps this was the court's fashion.

Her skirts flowed around her, the rich colors peeking out as she pranced around. The sleeves were tight along her shoulders and upper arms, then flared out right above her elbow, draping over her forearms and brushing almost against the floor with her skirts. How could anyone move with such long sleeves? She laughed in delight. And now she would have a dress for the ball!

But how could she trust that a gift like this was only what it appeared—a dress and no more? What if the mage had performed some untoward magic on it? She flung the dress off, throwing it onto her bed. It piled together like ribbons of darkness made tangible. Was wearing this dress something she could risk? She fingered the lush fabric. Perhaps she could take it apart and sell it, then use the proceeds to buy something herself. She might not have enough money to afford a whole dress of this ilk, but she could at least cobble something together. Yes, that would be the plan. She unfurled the dress and hung it up fondly, shaking out the wrinkles. Even if she couldn't keep it, it was still a lovely dress.

If you had asked her before today, she would have staunchly told you her affections could not be bought. But maybe she had judged this Lord Varrock too harshly… she would have to find him at the ball and make amends.

7

Thousands of people lived in the capital city. The majority lived below the hill where the palace sat, and if they planned on attending the night's open ball, they had to walk up that hill to enter the palace. As Anslee walked along with Magda, she felt as if the two of them were in the middle of a colorful parade. Plumed ladies and gentlemen walked in all their finery towards the castle atop the hill. So many of them attended that they flowed over the walkways and into the street. Anslee had considered trying to rent a hansom cab to carry them up the hill, but now she was glad she had not. The revelry and good-natured attitude of the pool of people made it feel as if the ball had already begun. She spotted many familiar faces, including the freckled girl from the market who wore the thin metal chain that she had been so proud of. Anslee had debated wearing her own locket but had decided against it. She didn't want to give anyone the wrong impression of allegiance during a night she meant to take advantage of prospective suitors! She ducked behind the girl to avoid Robert, who was swinging his arms wide, dressed in olive-frilled finery. Did he intend to mimic one of his plants? All around her, people talked about what they would eat and who they would dance the night away with.

Thankfully, Magda had been right in anticipating that she would need more time to prepare herself this afternoon. She had curled her hair until it lay just right, then loosely pinned it back against her head. The walk had already worked some pins free, and a few wayward pieces whispered against her neck. She glanced sideways at Magda, admiring her own hair. Magda had loosely pulled the dark chestnut brown, barely streaked with silver, back into a large bun on top of her head. It wasn't nearly as tangled with ringlets as Anslee's, but she felt the elegant look suited the woman. They had both rimmed their eyes with dark kohl and rouged their lips lightly. She wasn't sure where Magda had found the emerald green gown that she now wore, and the woman hadn't offered an explanation. It fit a little snugly, and she wondered if it was the same gown she had worn all those years ago. Anslee hadn't asked for fear she would turn the question on her, and she still did not have an appropriate answer. She looked down at her own gown. Anslee had run out of time to sell Lord Varrock's gift and sew her own gown together, so with a shrug, she had slipped into this piece of finery with the thought that surely wearing it for one night couldn't hurt.

Magda hadn't asked where Anslee's elaborate gown came from, perhaps for the same reason that Anslee had not. While Magda's gown had sleeves as long as Anslee's, instead of a layered underskirt, her gown had a sweeping train, which she scooped over her arm to keep it out of the street's muck.

"No one to impress on the way there," she had explained. Walking along now, Anslee did not quite believe her as Magda received several side-eye stares from men walking with their wives, too cowed to make a more overt move, although one got smacked by his wife's fan after looking for too long. Magda winked at her.

As they walked, Anslee felt the magic of the land waking up around her. She would have denied this knowledge, but after her run-in the other night (if that had even happened), she wasn't able to deny it anymore. Vines growing along the tall buildings reached out, trailing after her as the horde crawled up the hill, closer and closer to the palace. It seemed the energy of the gathered townsfolk had piqued the interest of the land's native magic, and it trailed the crowd with invisible sparks of desire and chaos as they approached the castle. The peaks of the turrets were visible now. And they had lowered the metal and wood drawbridge to allow the townspeople access to the inner courtyard.

Shadows licked her heels with every step. Anslee looked behind her. She stood in the middle of those walking up toward the palace. She saw the women from the market who had discussed the roamers give her an evil eye and step around her. Did anyone else notice the shadows? Did they feel the icy chill of eyes watching them? Suddenly Anslee felt like she was part of a herd of deer being hunted and corralled into a corner for easier picking. She looked uneasily about her as passersby laughed among themselves.

Magda stopped and turned several paces ahead, realizing that Anslee wasn't next to her.

"Nervous? Lovesick?" she asked, her eyes kind.

It startled Anslee to be addressed with such sincerity by the woman known as the Queen of Sass. She supposed that would make her the Princess of Sass.

"Don't you feel... concerned?" Anslee asked. She wasn't sure how to put her fears into words. It felt juvenile to admit she was scared of the dark. She had never asked Magda about the shadow monster, convincing herself she had run out to confront a rabid dog and then let her imagination get the best of her.

Magda looped her arm in Anslee's, gently tugging her along.

"I remember my first ball," she started. "My one and only ball, I thought. There was a man I had hoped to impress." She gave Anslee a meaningful look. "I know a thing or two about young love."

"It's not that," Anslee protested, but Magda waved her off.

"You may not want to tell me who, but I know someone delivered that extravagant dress for you." She eyed the dark richness of Anslee's dress, and a wave of self-consciousness hit her. She blushed at her audacity to assume the other woman was obtuse enough to overlook such extravagance. "You could have hidden this or taken it apart and sold the gems... Instead, you wore it. Now, now," she tutted, suppressing Anslee's protests that she *had* in fact planned to sell it. "You have every right to do whatever you would like with a gift. And as a gift, you are not beholden to anyone who gave this to you." She stopped and faced Anslee, suddenly serious.

"You don't need to do anything you don't want to. No one has forced your favors with this," Magda said, looking Anslee in the eye. "So enjoy your night, my dear. Look for your mysterious young man. But if you need to leave... you find me. And we will go."

The icy chill that gripped her heart melted away, and she gave Magda a quick hug. The woman may be a knightly terror in the kitchen, commanding Anslee like one of her troops, but she had never felt more grateful for the fiercely protective older woman.

The gates of the palace loomed before them. Anslee had only a moment to appreciate the awe of the towering fortress before the crowd whisked her through the gates and up to the guards, stoically watching the guests. Their unsmiling gazes slid over all who passed through the gates.

A shiver slid down her spine, and Magda, noticing, leaned closer. "It's fabulous, isn't it? I am not sure if you've ever been this close to the palace, but do not be scared, girl. It's just regular people that live inside these walls, same as you and me." Magda placed her arm around Anslee and gave her a brief squeeze. Staring at the grim soldiers, Anslee had the distinct feeling that they were not like her. Anslee did not feel the need to correct the older woman. She didn't have Anslee's memories of guards raiding the camp, looking for her father... not content to leave until blood was spilled. She didn't think she could ever trust law enforcement again.

The mob dragged them onward until they had passed through the courtyard and into a grand entryway. It was more extravagant than any parlor she had ever seen. A mid-sized arena with pleasant greenery on the ground and chandeliers above reflecting the growing, living things. It was as if she had entered a perfectly coiffed tiny forest without all the steam of a greenhouse or the dirt and twigs of a forest. Gilded candle sconces were fixed on the walls every few feet and down the corridors as far as the eye could see. Metal vines twisted and soared above them, gems winking underneath a domed glass ceiling. Dark clouds swirled ominously beyond, casting a foreboding feel to the evening.

But the crowd pressed forward, uncaring of the thriving, living embellishments and the shadows that tried to reach down and grab them. They were here to eat, to drink, and to be merry! They raced down the corridor until the flickering candles gave way to larger and larger torches, and the greenery crawled along the walls with them before abruptly ending.

Anslee caught their excitement. The hall looked nothing like the forested wilderness she had grown up running through. Shadows lengthened between the sconces placed every few feet, throwing dappled light onto the passing crowd. The metal vines were bare of the wild liveliness she associated with the woods. *Oohs* and *aahs* sounded around her. Others must find the ambiance romantic, but they were fools. Anslee knew darkness could hide danger. She was eager to pass through this hall of death masquerading as unnatural greenery.

The townsfolk stopped once the harsh glass of the chandeliers and the bright flames of the white gold torches surrounded them at the end of the hall. They faced a closed pair of ceiling-height wooden doors. Their reflection gleamed back at them against the polished oak. Her future lay on the other side of this door. Handsome strangers would be behind this door, ready to whisk her away to start a new life together. All she had to do was find them. And woo them. She swallowed her unease. Surely beyond those doors, the palace would feel alive.

Anslee pushed against the doors. She and Magda had made it to the front of the crowd. They were the start of the show, she realized, the first people these rich strangers would see when the doors opened. Anslee threw her shoulders back and glared at the doors imperiously, willing them to open. Shadows danced under her toes as she leaned forward, eager to fly into her future. Trumpets screamed on the other side of the door, and her pulse ricocheted.

The doors swung open, inviting them in.

8

"Courtesy of the King and Queen of the Dracorian Mountains, you are cordially invited to enter the ball this night, the Eve of Midsummer. We celebrate our missing Princess of the past twenty years, and give thanks to the bravery and perseverance of our rulers during this time.

Enter, the townspeople of Capital City."

There was a moment of hesitation, then the crowd surged forward, and Anslee allowed the mob to push her onward. They spilled forward onto a wide platform that oversaw the entire ballroom. Gold-plated steps dropped on three sides to the ballroom's floor. Instead of lush greenery, organized opulence reigned here. The steps down to the ballroom were tiny, and Anslee wondered if she should take them individually or if she was supposed to hop down every other.

"The last time I was here, the fashion was to wear heels so high a woman could only take the smallest of steps without a cane or a man's arm. Made it quite easy to see who was available in those days." Magda chuckled softly, her breath a whisper against Anslee's ear and her hand attached to her forearm. "Be careful not to slip since those stairs are slippery as butter."

The two of them carefully started their way down the stairs. To her surprise, Anslee saw a few who were already in their cups stumble down a few of the steep stairs. If she hadn't been looking because of Magda's warning, she would not have noticed they were immediately escorted out via side doors. Was that the end for them? Forced to leave after a simple misstep? She whipped her head toward Magda, who raised her eyebrows and slightly shook her head to discourage her unspoken question. A vision of the stoic palace guards flashed through her mind as they safely reached the bottom, and Magda escorted her through the center of the ballroom.

Unlike the front hall, this room was icy, calculated elegance. Faux gilded plants, abstract white marble art, and colorful peacock feathers adorned every surface. The white marble felt sterile and lifeless. It was as if someone had squeezed the very life out of this room until the townspeople entered. The floor was tiled marble with a gilded pathway leading from the double doors to the empty thrones. She was also disappointed to find the room empty of any rich strangers.

"What's the point of inviting us to a ball if we're the only ones here?" she asked, annoyed. Her panic from earlier came back, and she whirled. Were they indeed being herded? Was this all a ruse to trap them?

"Anslee, what is wrong with you tonight?" Magda asked her. "I've heard of being lovesick, but you're acting with straight paranoia. Are you *that* scared of this man?"

"Just looking for drinks," she tittered, but the words came out pitched and twitchy.

As Magda frowned, she veered them to the left side of the dais to the serving tables set with opulent dishes. Tall tables were scattered around them, and small clusters of people mingled, awkwardly sipping drinks they had just been handed, unsure how to act when they weren't the ones serving. She watched other locals enter the ballroom and scatter like seeds for the picking. None of them were good enough to be picked by her. Magda set Anslee up at a table and left to grab some delicacies for the two of them. A servant passed by and, with a slight bow, offered a sparkly glass filled with a bubbly, pale pink liquid.

"Rosé, miss?" he asked with a bow. She took two glasses.

"One is for my companion," she blurted out, immediately berating herself. Stupid, stupid girl. You could have just taken two glasses without bumbling about it. But the servant only nodded his head agreeably before wandering off to find other empty-handed guests. She took a sip of rosé, her first one ever, she thought giddily and set the other champagne flute down, determined not to stand there holding two glasses and looking as if she was already into her own cups. She was used to having a glass of town ale or two occasionally, but nothing as delicious and luxurious as this drink.

Magda came back as she was holding the glass up, looking at the bubbles. "Is it magic? How the bubbles form? Or something to do with the glass? Is this real crystal?" Anslee asked, intrigued.

Magda laughed at her. "If only. No, to the magic, of course not. That's been outlawed ever since the royals tucked themselves away in this castle."

Anslee wondered if the odd mage about town had known that. Was he unintentionally breaking the law? Or did he just not care?

"And as if they would serve us on anything worth something. This is most likely fool's glass. You've heard of fool's gold, yes? It's the same. You'd be a fool to take it and think you could pawn it." She gave Anslee the side eye as if she knew that's exactly what she would do. "See here?" She pointed to a tiny inverted set of v's engraved on the bottom of the glass. "They've marked them, see? You'd be tracked and hanged for stealing from the king and queen. Don't try it, dear."

Anslee gently put her glass down. Just holding it made her nervous now. If they had escorted people out for tripping already, what would happen if she accidentally broke a glass? Or if they caught her taking one?

Anslee surveyed her surroundings, scoping out the obvious wealth of the room and the eligible young gentlemen within it. The thrones sat on a dais of polished wood, and the ruler's throne itself was a mixture of scarlet and gold. She spotted at least three available-looking young men a stone's throw away. They stood together in a group, unencumbered by any sisters, mothers, or other women. Too bad they were townspeople as well... their clothes were a bit too shabby and poor fitting to be anything but. She was after richer game tonight.

She hoped the official couriers would hurry and get here. She still planned on evaluating Avery tonight, but it never hurt to prepare backups. If he was truly a danger to her, then she wouldn't give him another thought. But if she had overreacted, and he was indeed an enviable target... then she had a much steeper social climb ahead of her than she expected.

People were still filling up the hall, the bright colors swirling together on the main floor. The room was so large she thought it impossible the entire room would ever be full. Beyond the people and even more empty space, wide tall windows were flung open into the evening. The sun was just beginning to wane, and the rosy and pink hues blinked over the outstretched forested landscape. Were the roamers back at camp, settling down for the night? Was Robin somewhere out there? *Snap out of it,* she scolded herself. *You're not here to dream about the past. You have your future to look forward to.*

Magda's loud guffaw brought her attention back to the room. That woman had found the butcher again, and his wife was nowhere to be seen! The two huddled over a table of minced meat, and Anslee was sure they were telling inappropriate jokes because of the gesturing and loud laughing that ended every sentence.

There was another person she eagerly found her eyes searching for, but she could not find him. The mysterious Lord Varrock who had briefly met and charmed her. She wouldn't have felt so disheartened if he had not then sent her this dress. This wretched, beautiful, glorious dress! Anslee was convinced she had judged him too harshly when they first met, and the longer she thought about his token of affection, the more her heart warmed toward him. She smoothed her hands over the front bodice, feeling the fabric slide beneath her hands. Under the light of a thousand glittering chandeliers, her own dress blinked back at her. The overhead lights pulled forth the twinkle of even more tiny gems that she could not see in the dim light of her own room—a glittering trail along the lower edge of her bodice, over her hips and dipping down the front, and again on her shoulder blades before disappearing down her arms, only to appear in a sprinkling burst again at the very edges of the sleeves fabric. She had thought the dress fantastic before, but seeing it here and now, she was in awe all over again. And to think someone had bought this for her! It must have cost a fortune. Had it been wise to wear it after all? Perhaps she should have worn one of her comelier dresses after all.

Magda finally returned with food, interrupting her thoughts. “Did you have a good time gathering snacks? See anyone I should say hello to?” Anslee teased.

Magda pretended none the wiser, “No, I do not think so. Look at this array of treats I’ve found! And to not have to cook any of it, mmmm.” She smacked her lips in appreciation, and Anslee wanted to laugh at the sheer absurdity of it. To think they’d end up here, eating food prepared by the King and Queen’s own personal chef! Her stomach growled, and she realized she was just as excited to eat as her companion. They dug into the food, relishing the savory parcels of meat and pastries delicately filled with cream and cheese, and spices. It all tasted heavenly, rich, and succulent compared to the coarse meals of her daily life. Before she knew it, Magda had flagged down another servant and grabbed them each a bottle of the sweet pink bubbles.

“Where are the King and Queen?” Anslee mumbled around a mouthful of pastries. “I thought this was their celebration ball? Shouldn’t they be in attendance?”

“They’ll be here eventually, after the rabble quiets down. You can’t expect them to just sit and watch while we stuff our faces, can you? This may be a feast for us, but it’s just like any other day’s fare to them.” She paused to daintily dab at her mouth with a napkin and brushed off the crumbs that fell on her bosom.

“If it’s a ball in honor of their missing daughter, you’d think they would at least want to show their faces,” she burst out, and Magda raised her eyebrows.

“It’s their ball. They can do whatever they want.” A faraway look came into Magda’s eyes, as if she was seeing things that weren’t really there. “You can’t imagine what it’s like to lose a child, Anslee. Parents all grieve in their own way. Twenty years missing...” She shrugged. “Perhaps this is their last way of giving up. Putting it all out there for us to know they’re finally moving on from their grief." The woman's sentiments touched Anslee. Magda never seemed vulnerable to her, but the drinks must be causing her to let down her guard.

While Anslee felt the beginnings of pity stirring her heart, Magda's spine straightened, and she pushed the conversation aside. "But this is a time for celebration, my dear! What a powerful nation to have survived and yadda yadda. Now, let us toast to our good fortune for living in the city so we can partake in the festivities!" She raised her glass flute, and Anslee obligingly clinked hers against it.

As if their conversation had drawn the entrance of the royal party, suddenly the trumpets were blaring again, and a liveried footman announced the first royal entrants, and then the next, and the ones after them. A perpetual line of royals, trumpeting, and announcements were blaring through the hall. Anslee wanted to let out a whoop, "Time to start this celebration!" She turned to Magda and gripped her arm in excitement, but the other woman had a worried look on her face.

"What is it?" Anslee whispered, wondering what new secrets she would learn tonight. Magda waved away her concerns, the emerald folds of her sleeves swaying, but stopped when she really looked at the earnest face gazing up at her. She sighed. "I've just got a bad feeling about this. Everyone being rushed in all at once? No King and Queen to be found? Let us hope they actually show up, and we don't get kicked out. It's never a good sign when they're not in attendance to oversee their rowdy nobles."

The ballroom became more and more packed, and Anslee realized it seemed so large earlier because it was practically empty. But now lords and ladies from the palace and neighboring nations were flocking in. She still had not seen her mysterious lord from the gown shop, but it had only gotten harder to search for him in the growing throng. What if he did not show up tonight? She fingered the edge of her gown. His reclusiveness only made her more determined to find him again. But she now doubted she'd get the chance to thank him in person. But perhaps that was also a blessing.

The absence of the trumpets' blaring was suddenly much more poignant than when their brassy noise had first started. People stirred uneasily and slowly quieted, staring up at the entrance doors high above their heads. The oncoming line of nobility must have ended, and everyone was milling about, gathering drinks. Quietly, liveried footmen were moving through the crowd, unrolling an elegant red carpet over the trampled upon golden path. They forcefully shooed off anyone who accidentally stepped on this aisle.

The trumpets punctured the crowd's murmurings, louder than before. Delicate musical notes of a flute choir floated over them, complementing the impactful trumpet blasts. The musical announcement cut forth suddenly, and the head herald stepped forward, announcing the next entrants with grand gestures:

"Lords and Ladies and Townsfolk of the Capital City of the Dracorian Mountains, I present your Royal Sovereigns, King August and Queen Clementine!"

Where he would normally step back and let the announcing trumpets overtake him, there was nothing except silence. It swelled with expectation, and the room collectively held its breath, waiting since the herald obviously had more to say.

"Lords and ladies and townsfolk of the Capital City of the Dracorian Mountains, we have gathered here today in memory of our missing Princess and treasured heirloom. We have grieved over her loss and our Royal Sovereigns have endured as best they can while continuing to lead our bright and vital nation onward. Well have we endured this trying time. You have been gathered together in honor of the strength that was shown these past twenty years, however"—he paused, gathering his breath for last sentence—"that time has now passed, and you are here to victoriously rejoice and celebrate the return of your missing Princess, Gracelyn Theodora Dracor, daughter of the Royal Sovereigns, King August and Queen Clementine Dracor, heir to the throne of the Dracorian Mountains!"

There was a collective gasp from the entire crowd. Nobody in attendance had expected this. Mouths dropped open in denial, tears dripped from the eyes of those who had long-lost hope, and the doors swung open for the last time as the returned Princess walked forward, flanked by and overshadowing both her parents. The King beamed with pride. The Queen's eyes leaked tears, though her smile stayed frozenly intact. The Princess herself, resplendent in a gown of deep gold and a crown of twisted gilded laurel leaves, stood proud and certain before her people. A ruler, ready to lead.

Anslee was too far away to make out her features. There was a shock of dark brown hair, overshadowed by a large, ornate golden tiara. So this was the real reason for the ball tonight... Anslee slowly clapped along with everyone else. Was her return related to the magic she had witnessed only days ago? Or was that just a coincidence? Would she be competition for any eligible young men? Anslee crossed her arms and scowled.

"Furthermore, our princess is pleased to announce a new competition. The historical gold and ruby crown of the Dracorian Mountains is hidden in the land somewhere, waiting for her return. Whoever finds this crown and returns it to our rightful rulers shall be granted a boon—our princess's hand in marriage!"

The crowd broke into rambunctious cheers, full of whistling and hollers. The cacophony was deafening. If the common folk had been silenced into a surprised stupor at her return, they were ecstatic at the idea of marrying into the riches that the noble family offered. The princess smiled benevolently and waved at the adoring crowd below her.

Anslee froze, her memories stirring. A missing gold and ruby crown...

9

The late afternoon sunlight cast a hazy glow on their surroundings, and dust motes drifted in the air. Despite the warmth of the afternoon sun, a chill crawled up her spine. The giant trees cast long shadows, shifting as soon as she walked past. Every trunk became a foxhole where an enemy could be lurking. She whirled, and a shadow escaped her, but there was only the sound of her own breathing.

"Robin, does this place feel strange to you?" she asked, edging closer to him. They had been running in the Mistwoods to escape the feel of their hungry bellies before they had stumbled into this clearing.

He sat up from where he had fallen and looked around. "Strange? Not any more so than you cheating to win a race." He brushed off her concerns the same way he brushed the dirt off his jacket. But his eyes twinkled, and she knew he was only teasing her.

"I'm serious, Robin," Anslee said, careful to keep her voice down. She rubbed her hands against her arms to tame the goosebumps that had popped up all over her skin.

At the worry in her words, Robin jumped to his feet and slowly turned, taking in the massive trees and underbrush that trailed through the forest like veins on a person's skin.

He must be noticing the clearing was completely empty of the normal forest sounds made by happy animals nearby. The same silence Anslee had noticed. The silence of a predator looming nearby.

Robin shrugged off his unease and grabbed Anslee's hand, heading back up the hill. "We should head back. It's late, and I don't want to miss supper." The mirth was gone from his voice now.

Anslee charged up the hill after Robin but pulled away when she noticed something glinting underneath the foliage. The late afternoon haze brightened as she looked closer. Was her mind playing tricks on her?

Anslee ran back down the hill and dropped to the ground next to a tree trunk with a sizable clump of leaves underfoot. Was something metal in there? She forgot her unease as her search became more frenzied like a phantom had taken over her hands. She lost control of her movements, flinging leaves with abandon, and crawled around the trunk on her hands and knees, convinced that if she could just find whatever she was looking for, then she would know—

"Anslee! Lee!" Robin snapped her out of her trance. "Answer me! I've been shouting your name, but you haven't responded."

"Sorry," she mumbled, barely aware of his shouting. She heard him as if through a fog. "I have to find it..."

He knelt next to her. "What is it? Did you lose your dagger?"

"No, not the dagger." Robin was referring to the gift that her father had given her on her tenth birthday. Her father had been clear that a young woman was always to be prepared, and the small hilt wrapped in supple leather and carefully oiled to a shine had been made to fit perfectly in her small hand. Still kneeling, Anslee brushed her fingers over the top of the hilt that she had slid into her boot, confirming it was still there.

"Something metal. I don't know what, but something's definitely here."

Robin glanced around at the darkening surroundings. Though they stood in a patch of light from the setting sun, the silence still loomed. Anslee was too captivated by her digging to notice Robin's shiver before he started digging with her. He wanted them far from this place and quickly. The sooner he helped Anslee find what she wanted, the sooner they could leave.

They rooted through the leaves in an ever-widening circle. Grab. Brush. Throw. The repetitive motion furthered Anslee's frenzied state. Until her hand pricked something sharp, and she pulled away, blood dripping across her palm. Either that was a thorn or—she pushed her hand back in the pile, cautious this time, and closed her fingers over a thick metal band. She pulled it out and stared at a gold crown. She gasped and clutched the crown tighter. Blood dripped through her clenched fists and down her arm in narrow streams.

Rubies encircled the metal band, spaced evenly apart with small sapphires dotted them. She had stabbed herself on one of three pointed tines. The whole crown gave off an unearthly glow, reflecting on their faces, and even the dirt still clinging to it, now anointed with her blood, could not diminish its beauty. She gently grasped it with both hands, turning to show Robin what she had found.

10

Someone bumped into Anslee pulling her from her memory, and her glass of rosé sloshed over her drink and onto her dress. She couldn't spend one more second worrying about the crown. It caused her all sorts of anxiety and stress, and it would ruin her good night. And she was determined to have a good night. But everywhere she went, people were talking about the news. Snippets of conversation floated past her as she weaved between bodies.

"But where was she?"

"Who found her?"

"Is she even real?"

"Who cares! The drinks are real!"

Anslee could not separate the dancing from the gossiping from the celebratory crying of nobles and townsfolk alike. The common theme was disbelief. It seemed nobody expected this surprise announcement, and a ball that was setup to be a bittersweet occasion turned into a raucous celebration. Just as likely as the excited well-wishers were those who thought something darker was afoot.

Anslee, for one, sided with the naysayers. But she wanted to be a young woman in love tonight, not someone obsessed with conspiracy theories.

"I hear she's an imposter!"

"That's heresy," another hissed.

"Magic brought her here. Don't you know it's been seeping through the town borders?"

"Hush with this talk of magic. You'll get us thrown out!"

Anslee sped away from those conversations. She didn't want to be anywhere near this group when the eagle-eyed guards arrived to remove them. Anslee danced away with the frenetic energy of one trying to forget her past. But even on the dance floor, there was a distinct divide in the revelry. There was live music and mingling between the haves and the have-nots, though it was harder to tell from far away the distinction between the handmade gowns that had been worn several times from the brand-new gowns that were never worn before tonight. Close up, the differences were obvious. Bright colored pieces lovingly washed could never mend the frayed edges or faint fuzzing that appeared on the well-worn gowns.

Still, that did not hold back the revelry of their owners. Anslee danced the spectrum of the common village dances on the ballroom floor where the townsfolk had gathered. No matter how she tried to force it from her head, thoughts of the crown floated through her mind. Large circles, large movements, skipping about from person to person. No tiny details to obsess over. Colorful fabrics flashed before her eyes, mixing with the gold and garnet memories of a long-forgotten crown. These were exuberant dances meant for laughter and enjoyment, much different from the tightly controlled, close-knit parades the nobles danced before the royal dais. If she twirled hard enough, maybe her memories would spin away too.

After the last twirl, Anslee tore herself away from the dance floor. She searched for Magda, swiping another bubbly rosé from a servant passing by—anything to quiet her mind. The stain from her spilled glass had dried long ago. She spied Magda tucked away in a corner, flirting outrageously with someone Anslee could not see, though she'd bet anything it was that gods-forsaken butcher again. It wasn't her place to say anything, but she did not know what magnetized the two toward each other. Imagining how much she would be welcome to intrude in that conversation (not at all, she knew), she instead decided it was time for fresh air. She scooted along the edge of the ballroom toward the grand double wide windows that she had seen earlier. The sun had set after the announcement of the king and queen, and the sunset she had briefly glimpsed was long gone. Since then, someone had pulled thick drapes across the open doorways, trapping the warm, stale air inside. She slipped through the parting edges of one of these drapes and eased herself onto the shallow patio. Only a handful of other people were already outside, and those were too far away to talk to.

Strong pillars supported the walls, made of the same gleaming marble as the ballroom floor. It had been just as hard on her feet as she thought it would be, and she leaned against a pillar, letting the inky blackness envelop her and closing her eyes a moment, and letting her feet relax. Imagine having the sort of life that includes dancing against this hard floor every night! But then she'd certainly be able to afford a personal masseuse for daily foot massages as well. *Ah,* she sighed blissfully. *What a life that would be!* What a night to imagine such a life. She gave herself a few more minutes of respite, appreciating the music drifting out to her and the brief relapse from the hot crush of bodies.

She slid around the pillar she had been leaning against and almost ran into a man dressed in navy crushed velvet. He was eating a fresh fruit with gusto, not heeding the juices dripping down his chin. Anslee felt as if she was interrupting a very personal moment between this man and his fruit, and her unease heightened when he straightened upon seeing her. She had never seen this fruit before and stood transfixed as she wondered what delicious pies Magda could make with this. It was a deep red color that looked like a cross between an apple and a turnip. It squelched like a peach, and its sweetness dripped down the man's fingers and just touched the edge of his shirt sleeves. Juicy red seeds scattered over his vest. Perhaps that was the reason for his dark-textured suit if he always ate so sloppily?

The man dragged out a handkerchief from an inside pocket, staining it as he wiped his chin.

"You, ah, missed a bit, right there," Anslee pointed a gloved finger towards his left cheek, and he wiped at it again with his stained kerchief.

"Have you never had a pomegranate, dear? The arils are pesky things, getting everywhere. But they are so delicious, aren't they?"

He went to take another bite. With the pomegranate midway to his mouth, he stopped as if just noticing her silence. "Ah, you must be one of those villagers who thought they were actually invited to this thing." He wagged his finger at her. Anslee scowled. She *had* been invited, same as him! She was about to tell him so when he took a threatening step toward her.

"I almost mistook you with that fancy dress of yours, but you're really no better than the rest of them, are you?" He pushed himself off the wall and stalked towards her, throwing the half-eaten fruit at her. "Here, eat the rest of this. May as well learn something and engage in some culture while you're here."

Anslee jumped to the side too late, and the half-eaten pomegranate brushed against her dress, smearing the lovely color with deep red juices. Rage simmered hot below the surface, but she couldn't lash out at a noble. She knew better than that. She turned sideways and kept her eyes downcast, hoping he would mistake her anger for meekness. Holding her skirt out, the juices dripped to the floor as she debated how to salvage the dress.

She ripped off her gloves to blot the stain when the shadow of a man slid over her shoulder. Had that buffoon circled back to make her feel even worse? Her mouth curled back in a grimace, and she clenched her teeth to keep angry tears from spilling. Who cares if he had more money than her? Did that somehow give him the right to make her feel less than she was? Hot rage began to bubble over.

Her stain-cleaning antics forgotten, she jerked her head up to tell him exactly what she thought of a pompous old man throwing leftover fruit skins at another human being and ridiculing them at a party where they were both guests, but she slammed her head into someone's chin. She stumbled, hands gripping her head.

"Ow, ow, ow. What the gods?! Isn't it bad enough that you already—" She looked up and noticed this was not the same man who had been mocking her earlier. *Oh no, oh no, oh no.*

It was Avery.

For once, she found herself speechless.

"Were you expecting someone else?" he asked her quizzically, tilting his head. She jerked her head, but the pompous man with the damn pomegranate was gone. Her anger flared before softening slightly. Either Avery had scared off that rude man, or he had slipped away before Avery had noticed him.

"Ah, my apologies, milady." And he dipped down into a deep graceful bow, his wavy raven hair falling forward, and color flooded Anslee's cheeks. He looked resplendent in a deep plum color, offsetting his tanned skin, and she forgot she was supposed to be wary of him.

"You may not remember, but we met last week in a shop down in the city. I've been quite busy with work, which has unfortunately kept me from seeking more of your acquaintance." The very air darkened around them. Shadows rose as if to cover them from any eavesdroppers. Anslee suppressed a shiver at the sudden chill.

Forgotten? How could that even have been possible? Did he forget this dress he had sent to her? And what would he think about how she had failed to take care of it? He had dripped her in gems, and she had splattered them with juices. Her face burned.

He straightened. "I see you remember me then, by the look on your face. How do you like your dress? Luckily, I found just where to send it to you." His lips peeled back to show his perfect white teeth, and Anslee melted into a puddle of awe and desire. Adrenaline spiked as she re-considered her desire to find him again. She was playing with someone dangerous, but charming. She dipped into a brief, modest curtsy, pulling the side of the skirt with the stain behind her, gripping her skirt tightly. She couldn't let him see that.

"Of course, I remember you, Lord Avery. And I am just a 'miss,' no lady about it. Although I am sure you've found that out once you realized where I lived." She could not help but tease him a little, although there was also a serious undercurrent to her question.

He cocked an eyebrow. "You've said nothing about your dress. Is it not to your liking?"

Her breath hitched. Was he mocking her? Or mad at her? Had he noticed the stain? "This dress is... extravagant. Of course, I thank you for it. But I cannot help but wonder why you would send me something... worth so much after only just meeting me." Was it wise to tease a mage? She had a horrible sinking sensation. Oh gods, what if Magda had been right, and by wearing this dress out in public she had given some secret sign? That she was his for the taking and would have to go home with him tonight? *Oh gods, oh gods, oh gods.*

"Because you appreciated a similar dress so much in the shop. I knew you would cherish a gift like this. You'll forgive me if I took some creative liberties. The other was much too"—he waved his hands in distaste—"just too much fabric? I thought this one much more elegant, much more befitting... you."

Anslee bit her tongue, wiping her over-imaginative mind from the thoughts of his wandering hands and the liberties she had briefly assumed he would take with this dress. Desire ran through her veins at the thought. He reminded her of a barely tamed animal, eager and snapping. Good to know that had emphatically not been the case. It seemed the expense of this dress had not even occurred to him. Perhaps he would make a suitable lure, mage or no. Excitement danced through her at the thought.

"But you like it?" he persisted, tilting his head towards her as laughter spilled from the revelry inside.

"I do not believe I've ever received such a praiseworthy gift before. I adore it, and thank you for it." She gripped her hands tightly, reminding herself that it wasn't wise to play with wild animals. Even if she wanted to give him the benefit of the doubt.

He leaned back on his heels, obviously pleased with himself and his choice.

"Although I appreciated the card your note came in just as much," she continued. "Was that your artwork on the front?" For as beautiful as the dress had been, it took much more time and effort to have delicately drawn her name. And while she had hidden this dress away in the closet and even considered selling it, the artwork had been for her alone. She had proudly tucked it into the edge of the small mirror leaning above her dresser. *That* could still be appreciated, even if *he* must be forgotten.

His eyes widened at her question. She had surprised the beast. "Yes, of course, I wrote that. You appreciated that so much?" He crossed his arms, considering her, and she wondered if she should have shown more appreciation for the expensive gift and less for the free card that came with it.

"It was beautiful and so thoughtful. It must have taken more time to draw my name on that artwork than it did to pick out this dress." She fanned out the edges of the dress as she spoke of it, and a blush crept up his neck as he loosened his collar awkwardly.

"Yes, yes. It took some time to create that. I did not expect you would enjoy it so much, though." His smile dazzled, and she realized he was pleased with her answer. Butterflies took flight in her stomach. So he, too, had cared more about the card than the dress that came with it. Perhaps the dress had been an excuse to gift her with the other? Why was he making excuses to see her, anyway?

"There seems to be a party in there." He gestured airily with his hand, indicating the ball and revelry they had left behind the curtain. "Perhaps you would still do me the honor of a dance?" The sounds of laughter and music wafted over them as if there had been a vacuum in the space the two of them occupied, and she was just now noticing the noise.

Her instincts yelled at her to decline his outstretched arm, but she couldn't think of a reason that wouldn't offend him. She tentatively placed her fingertips onto his, and he tugged her forward. As he parted the curtains to let her step through, she realized they matched in their plum attire. She wondered if that had been on purpose as Avery pulled her through the crowd, which slowly parted for them. She felt like a jewel being shown off on his arm, her stains long forgotten. She breezed through the throng of people easily, feeling none of the crush of bodies surrounding her, and suddenly they were on the dance floor.

But not the townsfolk revelry that she had been part of before. This dance held the tight formations of the noble's dance floor. Stirrings of panic threatened to rise in her chest. She had never mastered any of these more formal dances. A memory of her last dance so close to a man flashed through her mind, Robin's face swimming in her memories.

Avery leaned forward and whispered in her ear, "Do not worry. I will lead, and none will ever know you did not grow up dancing on your toes."

The music started, and he gathered her in his arms, her breath hitching, and they were off. To her surprise, she recognized the music and steps and relaxed in his arms, her breathing smooth and even. The sudden awareness of the heat of his palm across her lower back and the warmth as he clasped her other hand made her feel impiously close to him. She had never let another man so close to her before, and suddenly she felt trapped. His warm breath brushed against her cheek as he spoke to her.

"You aren't nearly as bad at this as I'd thought you'd be, given your tense stance," he commented. She suppressed a shiver as his words caressed her. *Never let the predator recognize you as prey*, whispered a soft voice in her mind.

"I've practiced this one before, my lord." She didn't tell him she had been ten years old the last time she practiced these steps. He walked her to the crowded dance floor, but she had eyes only for him. With a barely concealed sigh of pleasure, she placed her hand on his shoulder. Shock ran through her, and it felt like they were trapped in a singular moment of time where just the two of them existed. He broke their bubble of silence.

"Now, now, do not start all that lord nonsense up with me," he told her, feigning shock. "We've already met twice, and exchanged gifts. We're friends now, my Anslee. Wouldn't you agree?" He looked her in the eye, and she blinked as if waking from a spell.

"You've given me several things, my... Avery," she stuttered over his name awkwardly. "But what have I ever given you in return?" They glided silently together, not touching another soul, though they danced in the middle of a crowd.

"Oh, many things, my dear. You just may not realize it." He twisted her in a spin, then captured her in his arms again. She had no time to puzzle his words. Did her budding friendship mean that much to him? Was this a reference to more mage tomfoolery? Although nothing he had done tonight indicated he even had the inkling of magic.

"Have you been enjoying the ball so far?" he asked.

"It's been amazing. I've never been to such a large celebration before," Anslee said carefully.

"Ah. And what a celebration it has been. Were you surprised by the reveal of the princess?" He eyed her intently, a shadow passing over his face at the mention of the princess.

"Of course. I believed everyone was." She glanced around them and lowered her voice conspiratorially, "Have you heard anything contrary?" She had thought she was teasing him, but his spine straightened underneath her hands, and his eyes darted around them. Surprised, she faltered in her step, and he had to catch her from tripping into another couple.

Looking at her wide eyes, his gaze softened, and his body posture loosened. "Of course not. It was a surprise to everyone except a tiny group of people. I expect only the king, queen, and herald even knew she had been found. Of course, as a steward of the realm, I was involved in her recapture." He spun her out and into a slight dip, covering her stumble at his words. He had been part of recovering the missing princess? And he was here dancing with her instead? Her pulse skyrocketed. Did that mean the crown had condoned the illicit use of magic to capture their princess? Uneasiness flooded her at the thought. She had wanted to bag a lord, all right, but not one so close to the crown!

He stepped back and bowed. "Thank you for the dance, Anslee. It was much appreciated. Unfortunately, I must return to my duties now, but I would like to call on you in the coming days. Will you receive me?"

She wanted to be overjoyed. This was just the sort of romantic interest she had hoped to kindle tonight. But her insides were frozen solid. He made her uneasy, no matter his calculated charm.

He smiled rakishly, and her heart skipped. "We are friends now, after all." He felt like the room they danced in—gilded and beautiful in the extreme but lacking substance. And the slight substance he had shown her - his closeness to the Dracor rulers - she didn't want any part in. But his eyes twinkled in the chandelier lights, as if daring her to turn him down. And she wasn't one to back down from a challenge.

"I look forward to your visit," she said formally. She meant to say more, but he turned on his heel and disappeared as the crowd shuffled her off the dance floor, and the music started again.

She wondered what sort of work he had to do that forced him to leave so suddenly. Was it related to his magic? Had he let any of it slip while they were dancing? She rubbed her arms vigorously, eager to remove any traces of it as the new dancers started up around her. The dances jostled her to the edge of the crowd, but she was fine with that. The fantasy of the evening had popped for her. Her new dress enticed no one except the person who gave it to her, but she worried he was slowly setting a snare that would spring around her neck when she least expected it.

11

It was time to leave. Her conversation with Avery had made her wary. She couldn't pinpoint why, but a feeling of unease permeated the air. The fruit man hadn't been the only one with rude manners. She heard snatches of other snarky conversations, and the lads were getting a little too grabby as she passed. Dances had turned wild and unruly. Drinks were poured with abandon, and whispers of the uncanny return of the princess were turning into uncontrolled shouts by belligerent drunks. The large crowd was taking on a mob-like quality.

Anslee slid through the crowd to Magda's side, who spilled her drink down Anslee's dress in surprise. Another stain. Lovely.

"And where have ye wandered off to, my wee lass?" Her accent was much thicker when she was tired or in her cups, and Anslee had an idea the latter caused tonight's burr. "Meeting and exciting all the young men, I imagine. But where are they?" She leaned forward and peered around the ballroom, looking for the hordes of men that she teased Anslee about. She hiccupped, and, thrown off balance, lurched sideways. Anslee yanked her upright.

"I think it's time we get you home, Magda. Where is that damn butcher when you need him?" she mumbled under her breath.

"Whas' that?" Green eyes, sharp and angry, flashed before her, and suddenly Magda's breath was in her face.

"Nothing. Let's get out of here." Anslee had them up the golden steps and down the hallway without the chance to appreciate the beauty and grandeur that she had admired on the way inside. Climbing the stairs leaning against one another was a little treacherous, and she had the distinct feeling the guards would have escorted them out if they were not already on their way out. Soon they were traipsing back down the hill they had walked up earlier that afternoon, dark and empty in the night time. Most of the revelry makers were still at the ball, not out causing havoc in the city streets, so they weaved down the middle of the street like drunkards. Anslee pulled Magda closer, wary of walking alone out in the streets.

"Did I ever tell you the story of the lost princess?" Magda slurred. She took off her shoes and, after considering them for a moment, decided they were much too heavy. They dropped to the ground.

"No." Anslee bent down to pick up the shoes, the hem of her dress trailing down the dirty street. At this point, the night had ruined the dress beyond repair. After three stains, it would take less time to rip about the gown and sell the gems for money than waste time cleaning it.

"Well, has anyone?" Magda persisted.

"I'm sure I've heard it." Anslee tried to keep this conversation brief. She wanted to get them home and to bed.

"You were young when it happened. But a babe yourself!" Magda practically shouted to the streets, and Anslee tried not to laugh as she shushed her. It was hard to fear unimaginable monsters when Magda was with her.

"Shhh! You'll wake the whole city!"

"I'll be damned to the gods! There's no one left to wake, lassie. They're all at that damn ball! Except that butcher... mmmm, have you ever gotten a good look at him? And when he bends over to pull out all that fresh meat for me—"

"Stop! Stop!" Anslee was almost in tears now, trying not to laugh. Gods, who wanted to picture that?

"Eh, he's not your type, hmm? Well, I'm sure you'll find a boy one of these days, and then that pretty little face of yours will not laugh at little ole me so much. Gots to get dressed up for someone, am I right? I know that dress did not get into your closet on its own. Perhaps you've already found someone after all." Magda narrowed her eyes conspiratorially.

"Weren't you telling me a story about the missing princess?" Anslee pressed.

"Not missing! Lost! Stolen!" The fabric brushed through Magda's fingers as she quickly dropped it and dramatically swung her arms. Again, Anslee was grateful for the silent streets during this drunken exchange. If those guards could see them now, we'd be imprisoned for heresy, even if Magda only spouted lies. But in a mood like this, it was best to appease her.

"And who stole her?" Anslee asked placatingly.

"Nobody knows. One day she was there, and the next, poof! She was not." Magda threw her arms wide in an invisible explosion, then shrugged. "And then, this is not as well known, but the crown was missing too." Anslee bit her lip so hard she tasted blood.

"A crown?"

"You know, one of those fancy circular pieces that go on your head? Made of metal? And jewels? Are you daft, girl?" Magda circled her hands around her head as if placing a golden circlet there. Anslee stepped closer, pulling Magda along by the arm. After the country's Dracor majesties announced the reward for such a missing crown today, she didn't want to become any thief's target.

"Are you sure about that?" Anslee asked in a low voice. "I don't remember any stories mentioning a crown."

"Quite sure. It was a secret part of the story. And an even more secret part," her voice dropped to the barest of a whisper, and Anslee could barely hear her next few words, "It's whispered that *they* did it. Beyond the mountains, to the east." Ice trickled down Anslee's spine. She had never heard any mention of these parts of the stories. Perhaps Magda was making this up to scare her for the night.

"No one lives out past the border, Magda. Everyone knows this."

"No, not people," Magda whispered.

"The land is just too wild," Anslee protested.

"For people," Magda insisted.

"What else would live out there?"

"Not animals, not people. Not gods..." Magda had stopped walking and stared off into the distance. Anslee had to prod her along. "No, not quite gods," Magda whispered, almost to herself.

This conversation was no longer funny.

"Magda, what are you talking about?" Anslee asked.

Magda's wide, luminous eyes reflected the moonlight.

"There are things out there. Not human, not animal... savage, wild things." Magda shrunk in on herself, as if her very words scared her.

Anslee wrapped her arm around Magda's shoulders. "There, there. I think maybe someone's had too much to drink tonight. Let's get home, where it's safe and sound. And you can have a nice, long sleep tonight. Does that sound good?"

Magda hiccupped and gave a small nod against her shoulder. She was quiet the rest of the way home and let herself be tucked into bed. Anslee barely heard the mutterings of the 'yonder monsters' as Magda turned over, and her mumblings turned into light snoring.

Anslee had wanted to steal the crown when she found it in the woods with Robin all those years ago, but Robin had resisted. She remembered chilly nights shuffling around fires, long days on the road, and the gnaw of hunger in her belly, which she could already feel rumbling again. Dismantling and selling a gem-encrusted crown for parts would have solved the problems of poverty for both their families—perhaps even the whole village! But she didn't have those concerns anymore. Now with a cozy bed and a roof over her head, there was more to fear from a local thief or smuggler. Perhaps Robin had been right, and that crown would have caused more trouble than it was worth.

12

Anslee was up with the dawn. A late night merry-making may have been a sufficient excuse for the lords and ladies of Yonderton to sleep in and waste the day away. But for a measly servant like her, there were still dishes to wash, meals to prepare, chamber pots to empty…

She sighed as she trudged forward with a heavy one in hand now. The smell was overwhelming. If she never had to carry someone else's shit as long as she lived, it would be too soon. If only Avery could see her now. He'd be regretting his fine words and good-natured smoldering.

"Awake and at work so early?"

She dropped the pot, splashing its icky contents all over her shoes, and whirled at the sudden voice behind her.

"Oh, you again," she said, backtracking and tripping over the pot she had just dropped, spilling its contents over the ground. Old urine and worse seeped underneath her skirts, wetting them.

Robin reached down to offer her a helping hand. "We need to stop running into each other like this." His eyes twinkled.

Anslee waved him off, pushing herself up to standing. This run-in was embarrassing enough as it was. She didn't need his help too.

"No, you need to stop surprising me," she scolded him. Her head pounded from too much drink the previous evening. "Look what you've made me do!" She pointed at the ground and glared at him. "Well, are you going to help me clean it up or not?"

He had the good sense to look sheepish, but he didn't back down from her challenge or mock her now ruined skirts. Or comment on how she now smelled.

He bent down, pulling a flat dagger from somewhere hidden on his person and scooped the contents back into the pot.

"Sorry about this, Lee. And after I came to ask a favor of you, here I am making more work for you."

Her ears perked up. A favor from a roamer? Now that was something that could come in handy.

He kneeled at her feet, finishing her chores. If she wanted, she could reach out and touch his softly curling hair. She yanked her hand back. Robin looked up at her and winked.

"I see I've piqued your interest. Now I have it on good authority that there was a ball last night—"

"Hard not to know. The whole town was there!"

He grimaced. "Not the *whole* city. Anyway, I learned that there is a reward to be had for discovering the crown..."

"I never took you as one eager to rule," Anslee snapped.

"You can't really think they'd allow one of *us* to sit on the throne," Robin replied.

She prickled at the use of the word *us*.

"No, surely, there will be an alternative reward for those they deem not suitable," he continued.

"No."

"No, you don't think there would be a reward?" He finished scooping the shit back into the pot and stood up, wiping his hands on a rag he pulled from his back pocket.

"No, I won't help you.""C'mon, Lee. You didn't even let me ask for my favor yet," he cajoled. He thought he was charming. He was. But she wouldn't be swayed.

"No, you know what that crown brought us last time we found it. I won't do it again."

"But what if I told you who it would help?"

"It only brings death," Anslee told him flatly.

"So you believe in superstition now?" he asked, an eyebrow quirked.

"Believing something you see with your own eyes doesn't make you superstitious," Anslee told him. "It makes you smart. Now get out of my way before someone comes looking for me." She stepped around him, and picked up the disgusting chamber pot. Too late she realized slop covered the handles. She gritted her teeth and kept walking.

Robin chased her, offering to help and pulling the chamber pot free until it tumbled down again.

"You came all this way to make my life harder, is that it?" she shouted at him, her temper exploding.

He recoiled as if he had been slapped. "It was an accident, Lee. Let me help..." They bumped heads as they bent down to pick up the pot at the same time. Anslee slapped his hand away, covering her forehead with a hand she realized too late was gross and smelly. Damn it.

"Any help you could have provided is long forfeit," she told him coldly.

"What do you mean, Lee?" he asked softly.

"It doesn't matter any more, Robin. Just leave me alone. Please. You know what finding that crown cost me." He regarded her silently. He pulled another rag from his pants. Where did he keep these things? But she had been a roamer once too... used to storing and stashing knickknacks on her person, never knowing what would be useful. He threw the rag to her, and she snatched it out of the air.

"Okay, I'll respect your wishes. You won't hear from me again." Robin gave a low bow, a mockery of what she had witnessed last night. His eyes no longer danced. "Nice necklace, by the way," he said softly before turning around and leaving.

Anslee remembered too late that she wore the thin silver locket he had given her. Her thoughts flashed to the freckled girl on market day, boasting about the promise chain she had been gifted. Had Robin thought things between them... No, that would be absurd. And even if that were true, she had just shut the door on any future possibility between the two childhood friends. No, Robin didn't fit into her future. He would stay in her past, where he belonged.

13

Magda surprised Anslee by bustling about the kitchen when she walked back inside. She herself felt exhausted by the late night, despite having much less to drink than her other half had.

"You seem bright and bushy-tailed today," Magda chirped at her. "I can barely tell you were up dancing till the wee hours of the morning." She looked up from her baking, eyeing her charge's disheveled appearance.

"You're one to judge." Anslee leaned against a wall, not attempting to help knowing the mess she was covered in. "That's probably because you don't remember the end of the ball or needing to be walked home and tucked in like a little babe." She tried to keep the sneer out of her voice, but she was tired from the late night and annoyed by Robin's request.

"Maybe I was asleep earlier, but it seems like someone else needs to find their way back to bed," Magda told her. "Come back down when you've taken your sass levels down a notch, girl." So said the Queen of Sass. She must be feeling the aftereffects of too much imbibing.

Anslee uncrossed her arms and made her way over to fill and heat a tea kettle before rifling through their teas. She pulled out her and Magda's favorite blend. She offered it in a silent peace offering. "Put it over there by the kettle. You can get out some snacks as well." She motioned to the delicate pastries that had appeared in the corner. Anslee did not know where or when they had come from, but she decided not to press the issue by asking. Who could turn down treats? "I'm sorry, Magda," she finally said, settling into Magda's worn-out corner chair. "I think I am just tired."

Magda gave her a tight-lipped smile. "Who isn't? I am not feeling too great myself this morning."

"Hopefully better than last night's paranoia. You were telling some strange ghost stories," she teased. The whistle on the tea kettle blew, and she meandered over to pour the steaming water into two mugs. "Do you really believe all that you were saying?"

Magda frowned. "Those were just old wives' tales. Don't listen to anything I say once I've been drinking." She tried to brush it off, but Anslee wasn't buying her overly dismissive tone.

"Oh my gods, Magda! You really believe everything you were saying last night?"

"Of course not! Now hush. Didn't I just tell you I wasn't feeling well? And here you are, yammering in my ear without a care in the world. As if I did not just tell you I need to sit here in silence and recuperate." She snatched her tea from the table. "Now, let us all hush for the rest of the morning."

It was later that afternoon when the butler poked his nose into the kitchen. True to their word, the two women had spent the morning in complete silence. "I have a message for Miss Anslee? Would you like to come retrieve it?"

"Yes, Thomas. I'll come pick up the message. And then I'll need to change as well." Magda eyed her over the fire, noticing Anslee's stains. She tried not to shake her head as she followed him out of the kitchen and down the hallway. Thomas stepped aside with a flourish, waving out his hand for Anslee to see the small card with her name inscribed on the front in elegant writing. Since no one ever came to visit their old master, this was one of the few messages Thomas had delivered. Otherwise, she would expect much less attention for such a little note.

She recognized the handwriting immediately and tried not to give herself away with any obvious gestures of excitement. Quick praise would be the easiest way to stave off his curiosity.

"Thank you, Thomas. I'll take this up to my room." She delicately snatched the card off the plate and turned to run up the stairs to her room, avoiding awkward questions that the young butler may have wanted to ask. Her name did not have the same delicate artistry that had existed in the letter that came with her last package, but the beautiful scrawl matched the writing inside the letter. She had expected to hear from Avery, but not so soon. Holding her breath, she paused a moment before sliding her nail against the seal and easing the letter out.

My dearest Anslee,

How lovely to see you at last night's ball. I regret that my duties prevented us from becoming better acquainted with one another. I hope you can forgive me for constantly running off on our time together. I plan to call on you tomorrow afternoon for a walk in the Grand Park, and would be delighted if you would accept. I am new in town and have much to learn of your ways.

Yours,

Lord Avery

She clutched the letter to her chest. Her excitement mingled with a foreboding sense of dread. What had she done to garner his attention? Had she simply been in the right place at the right time? She wanted to turn him down. She really did. But every time he cornered her, she felt compelled to answer him... to agree with him... Perhaps he didn't realize the effect he had on her and assumed she was another young woman happy to accept his advances. And if it had been any other magic-less man, she would have been! He was handsome, cordial, and obviously rich. But why did his touch cause the hair on the back of her neck to rise? And why did his smile remind her of a predatory cat about to pounce? She shuddered. No way around it, she'd just have to face him in person and tell him no. Or let Magda do it for her. She had offered before the ball, after all.

She placed the letter beside the decorated envelope he had sent to her before. His little gifts were cluttering her room, marking his territory. She swept them both into the wastebasket, claiming the room for herself again.

The trailing ivy by the window perked up, curling towards her hand like a cat wanting to be pet. She stroked it absently. *Magic couldn't be real*, she thought to herself. *It must be my mind overreacting again, as Magda is so fond of saying. Simply the imagination searching for adventure.*

"Are you done yet? There are chores to be done!" Magda called up the stairs.

Anslee slipped outside the door, and the vine stretched after her, falling flat. No, the chores could never wait. It almost made her reconsider Robin's offer to go after the crown. But that would be a fool's errand. And she was not a fool.

14

Avery

"This is a dangerous game you are playing, Varrock." His future queen's voice was quiet with anger.

"And not keeping your emotions in check is a dangerous game you are playing, *princess*." He emphasized the last word, taunting her. He did not like having his decisions questioned. She glowered at him.

"I keep them where they need to be kept. Which is out in the open when you are endangering our mission."

Avery sighed and turned his back on her anger. This deception would be easier to pull off if she would simply trust him. He had trained for this since birth. That's why he led their mission, even though she far outranked him.

"Oh, please. No one suspects you. I have made sure of that," he said snidely. "The first reports of harmed citizens have already started to trickle in." He looked back at her, his voice rising in anger. "And I will not have your emotions ruining what we have fought so hard to establish. So you sit on that throne and keep your mouth shut."

She opened her mouth to snarl at him some more when he cut her off with his last words. He had spent the last twenty years running this deception, and he would let the humans take back this land before he would cede control of his plans to *her*. "If you want to remain on the throne, princess, do not question my control, my rules, nor my methods. You were easily found, and you can be easily replaced. Do not forget what happened to the last princess of this land."

She sucked in a breath, her dark eyes open wide and her lips paling over her exposed canines. Her talon-like nails punctured the cushion of the velvet covered throne she sat upon.

"I am your Queen," she hissed. "Do not mistake that. You can never replace me, but I could dismiss you here and now if I wished it. Stop your playing, Varrock, and get back to work!"

He bowed, seething in silence. She might think Anslee was just a plaything to him, but he had plans for her... and he wouldn't let his queen sway him, no matter how much she blustered.

15

Anslee walked through the promenade with Avery, delighted that they could finally spend this time together. He had arrived at noon to retrieve her, and she had begged Magda for the afternoon off to see him. Despite her better judgment, his very presence enthralled her. Magda had teased her mercilessly about finally meeting the man who had footed the bill for the purple dress, but she had shut the kitchen door on her and escaped out the front before anyone followed her.

She cast her eyes sideways to admire his profile. He graciously pretended not to know what she was doing, and she blushed at thoughts she would not want him to read. He wore a suit of dark navy today, with mahogany brown boots brushed to a rich shine, and a cream-colored shirt with a slight ruffle at the neckline. Perfectly inappropriate for anything except lounging. Her dress, however, was a bit more practical. She did not own nearly as many clothes for casual elegance as she was sure he did. Certainly nothing like the purple gown from the other night! She had a modest pale blue gown with gauzy fluttered sleeves. A pale yellow shawl covered her arms for propriety and matched the patterned pastel yellow and pink tulips that bordered the skirt and bodice of her dress. Perfectly acceptable for a stroll in the park.

The city was in mid-summer, and a light breeze drafted over them from the nearby lake. It was warm for the shawl she wore, but she pulled it tighter, self-conscious about her humble attire when they walked past ladies dripping in the newest fashions. The fanciest thing she wore was a matching hair ribbon, keeping her hair pulled out of her face.

The walkways in the park were full of other young couples and families, likewise diverting themselves as Anslee and Avery had set out to do. They passed a ground of young men teasing one another about being harassed by wolves around the forest's edge. Anslee shivered and pulled her shawl closer. She didn't want to think about *that* today.

Avery had asked her to accompany him this afternoon by claiming her as a tour guide. Since she had grown up in the capital, he reasoned, she must know the best haunts. He offered his arm with a smile, and she gallantly took it. She ignored the little voice inside her, insisting he could play with magic as only the dangerous could.

"So this must be the infamous Capital Park. I had heard it was the original battleground the royal family stood upon when they first claimed this land." His voice was light and jovial, contradicting his almost bitter words.

Anslee laughed uncomfortably, "Now that's a story I had not heard before." She had assumed he would ask about the pond or what social activities to look forward to in the height of summer. She had been prepared to talk about the city's festivals, feeding the ducks, or something more banal—not war.

"I am surprised they do not keep a little summary of it hidden beneath the name. Apparently, this land used to belong to the creatures to the east of us," he gestured airily with his free hand.

"'Creatures'?" she asked.

"The creatures are not like the people of this land, or so the stories say."

She wondered what stories he spoke of. Certainly none that she had heard.

"Aren't you from the east? Perhaps that is why you've heard of this story, and I have not. Am I hearing a little of the local flavor, perhaps?"

"Perhaps," he answered noncommittally, giving her a grin. "Anyway, the people of this land allegedly came to the battleground armed to the teeth and demanded the passive creatures leave their dwellings immediately, or they would suffer the consequences. Not wanting to start a battle and fearing for their lives, the villagers fled, leaving all of their possessions behind. It's said they have been building armies and strategizing for their return since that day, convinced that their peaceful way of life was their downfall." He stared off into the distance. She wondered where he had heard that fable. It certainly wasn't part of the fairy tales that she had grown up hearing.

"That is certainly a morbid story. Not one that I have heard spoken of in the rest of the kingdom." She paused, contemplating his words. "Is that what you tell your youngsters to keep them in bed and out from wandering the dark streets at night?" Her tone was light, but she wondered how much of that story he believed. Was he secretly a militant? Was that why he practiced magic?

"It is what our elders tell their successors. What our kinsmen whisper in the streets. It is their truth that one day, the east will rise again and take back what is theirs." He stated this so matter-of-factly a shiver crawled up the base of her spine, despite the bright sunshine and cloudless sky above them. A whisper of the stories Magda had been telling her the other night fluttered through her mind.

"Are you cold, my dear?" He looked down at her as if he had felt the goosebumps prickling up her covered arms and spine. She smiled up at him, mentally banishing all traces of unease.

"No, of course not. Thank you for asking, but it's quite a lovely day out. I could not possibly be cold, but it's kind of you to be so concerned for me." He patted her arm and drew her closer. She was grateful for her shawl now because it kept their skin from touching.

"And what else can you tell me of your life?" he asked her. "You live on the Warwick Estate? And how are you related to that old lord?"

A blush rapidly spread across her cheeks. So it was time for the truth to come out after all.

"I am not related, my lord." She hesitated. "I am just a servant that the lady of the house was once fond of, that's all. I've lived and worked at the Warwick Estate ever since I was a child."

"No relation then?" He raised his eyebrows slightly, and she winced, waiting for the verbal blows to land.

"No. Does this disappoint you?" She held his arm tentatively as if their whole relationship was about to unravel before it had a chance to begin. She lifted her skirt lightly, pretending there was a puddle she did not want to dip her skirts into. It gave her something to do with her hands so they weren't just awkwardly dangling by her sides when he inevitably pulled away.

"Of course not." His grin softened the harsh angles of his face. "I knew there were no young noblewomen living there. I just know it's not uncommon for a distant relative to go work for one that's more well off. If that is not how you came to be here, what else can you tell me about your past? Have you always lived in this city?"

She wanted to slap her palm against her face. Out of the frying pan and into the fire, wasn't that the saying? Being a servant was one thing, but learning her true birthright as a roamer... no, that would never be accepted in finer society. Her company was fit for thieves and murderers only.

"No, I haven't always lived here," she started off tentatively. "I used to... move around with my family often. But after a.... a freak accident, they sent me to serve the Lord and Lady Warwick, as I do now." If he noticed the odd pauses in her explanation, Avery was too kind to point them out. Doubtless, he would feel like an ass if he pushed her to explain more about such an uncomfortable past.

"Did you ever wander near the eastern lands? Perhaps, we have met before?"

"No, we never wandered that way. We always ran to the west, but not so far as the coastal regions. We never ventured out east. The woods... just weren't as friendly out there." Her explanation faltered off. "Not that... I am sure they are lovely," she hurried to correct her mistake. "I mean, I would not know personally, never having been there. But I am sure they are just lovely to be in. Do you miss your home?"

There were a few moments that Avery had time to think of his answer as a rather large, rambunctious family walked up to them on the opposite side of the promenade. They had to veer to one side of the walkway and walk side by side so as not to run into the noisy children zigging and zagging around. Avery frowned at them, as if annoyed at the playing. Anslee frowned at Avery's frown. Who dismissed merry children so readily? After her childhood, she would cherish any children she had the pleasure to be around. Their lives were hard enough.

"Of course, I miss my homeland. Who would not?" Avery said. "But it's a rare treat for me to be in the Capital. I never planned on staying away forever; I hope you realize. Everyone deserves to return home."

They fell into a morose silence. Where was her home? She had lived here for years, but would she really call this existence a home? As a child, home had been a feeling of belonging—knowing someone was searching for you at dinnertime, looking out for you when you did not have any friends. Never an actual physical location. They had moved around too much for that. She wondered if maybe her perception of having a home had changed. Instead of a specific person, it was a safe haven where you returned after a long day.

A fortune teller was just around the bend, offering a brief game of chance or a reading of your future through your palms. Anslee winced, but Avery did not see her. Speaking of home, this vision itself was a reminder of her past. Some women from their traveling village would pretend to be fortune tellers. They had intrigued her, until one of them had read her past as one of cobwebs and inky nothingness and nonexistence, and terrified her enough that she had sworn them off altogether. Old Ross had been furious when he had heard, and tried to get the woman kicked out of their caravan. She sighed. None of that story would ever have gotten out if he had not found her crying in a corner, trying to get all her tears out before he or Robin found her.

Avery remained oblivious to all these thoughts running through her head. He stared transfixed at the roamer woman down the row, her fuchsia and purple shawl wrapped around her—a fortune teller's trademark. She sat at a small table with a forest green covering and her weapons of choice laid out before her—a crystal ball, tarot cards, and even tea leaves for steeping and draining.

"We should go see her." Avery tugged slightly on her arm to hurry her forward. It was the most interested she had ever seen him look at something, even her. Anslee wondered if she should feel put out that another person was intriguing him more than her, but she could not muster up any sort of jealous emotion. She had lived that life. She had seen those women. She had no desire to return to it, and the trials and heartache that accompanied it.

"Have you ever had this done before?" he asked, his eyes bright with excitement. "I have heard of it but never tried. What a strange sort of magic these women must possess in order to discern things kept secret from all else except the gods."

Her insides froze, but she shrugged noncommittally. Fortune tellers were con artists, everyone knew that. Except he believed in magic.

"I think most of them are frauds," she said icily.

"Oh, come now," he laughed at her. "Show a little faith."

She pursed her lips, but said nothing else. She didn't want him to learn her true feelings about roamers.

Avery dragged her down to the fortune teller's tent.

"Hello, my children of the world." The woman greeted the two of them with a smile and downcast eyes. She wore a black headdress, simple in its colors but deceptively intricate the closer she could see it. It was made of the lightest fabric that swooped and overlaid on itself, coming down to cover the front part of her hair, forehead, and eyes. Only if one sat across from her would they be able to see the woman's eyes. Anslee tried not to scoff and roll her eyes. Apparently this cheap trick worked on some people; Avery still seemed smitten. She tried to distance herself and step away while he fulfilled his fantasy, but he continued to pull her forward with him.

"I have never met a woman of the fortune before," he explained to her. "I have to admit it makes me feel nervous." He pulled at his collar, laughing half-heartedly. Anslee frowned, but the roamer smiled gaily.

"As well it might, young man. I have been around the nation reading fortunes bearing both good and ill tidings. One never knows how the gods will determine their fate."

Avery bobbed his head in agreement. "I am eager to know what you can tell me, but as I mentioned, I feel a bit uneasy. Perhaps, my companion can have her wishes told before me and ease my concerns. I am sure, my dear"—he pulled Anslee forward to the empty chair placed opposite the fortune teller—"that you could oblige me this one small request?"

She remembered the conversation about the give and take of their being friends and wondered if this was one of those tiny things she was supposed to "give" to him. She hesitated for a moment before letting herself be pulled down into the seat. She wondered if the roamer was blind or just unconcerned, as she seemed totally immune to their disagreement. Anslee suppressed a sigh as she succumbed to her fate.

"The cards do not speak to me for free," the woman continued, still not looking at them.

"Of course," Avery acquiesced, taking a large chunk of change and clanking it on the table. Anslee looked at that lump sum with round eyes. Did he even realize how much worth he had just thrown on the table? He was grossly overpaying for this fake's services.

The clanking of change caused the woman to jerk her eyes up. Eyes that Anslee recognized stared back at her over the crystal ball. Anslee froze, terrified. This woman had been one of the traveling roamers she grew up with. In fact, she had been the daughter of the very woman who had terrified Anslee as a young child.

Recognition dawned in the roamer's eyes, and she wondered if her charade with Avery was about to officially come to a close. She scowled, warning the other woman off recognizing her aloud. Yes, she had come clean with Avery about being a servant, but if he learned she used to be a homeless heathen herself, that she traveled from place to place and lived in the dirt her entire childhood? Why, he was so enamored with this roamer that he might just lock Anslee up and return her to the east forests from which he came.

The woman—Cria, Anslee remembered with a start—tilted her head, mouthing the words, *Does he know?* Anslee was suddenly grateful for the fortune teller's ridiculous veil, which hid her moving lips. She subtly shook her head. If Anslee was still a roamer, she wouldn't be ambling up in a maid's garb hanging on the arm of a lord. Anslee blushed at her foolishness. How could she ever have assumed they could be anything more?

Please don't give me away, she begged.

The woman placed her hands against the table and rose. She flung her arms up and stared Avery in the face.

"The gods have accepted your donation! Go, and return once we are complete!"

He scowled, and Anslee's breath caught. Her thoughts flashed to the magic she had seen him perform at the dress shop, and the brief glimpses of wildness he had let slip during the ball. She was reminded of the predator he had seemed, and she took a step away.

"But I thought I was to watch and observe?" Avery continued, unaware of Anslee's small step backward. "After all, that is how I will be assured that my fortune's reading will be accurate as well."

"The fate is between the gods and those who select to speak with them. It is not for prying eyes and ears," Cria said. "You can wait your turn, and then I may speak to you privately if you so desire." She sat back down, dismissing Anslee's date, who sulked off a respectable distance away. He crossed his arms and glared.

She huffed down in her seat. "Good gods, Lee. You sure know how to choose them! That one's a looker, for sure, but he's got the attitude of a jackass."

"He wasn't so bad before," Anslee whispered, not letting the shock of her old childhood nickname show on her face. She had gone ten years without hearing it, and now it'd been spoken aloud by two people in so many days.

"You must just have that effect on men," she teased.

They grinned at each other. Anslee debated asking her about Robin before remembering she had decided he belonged in the past.

"It's been too long, Lee," Cria murmured. "Where have you been all these years? Truthfully, I assumed you had died, and then possibly never existed, and

I had imagined that honey haired child wandering around our camps." That sentiment creeped her out. It was eerily reminiscent of what Cria's mother had told her long ago.

"I've just been living here in the city. I assumed you knew?"

"No, no one told me. I haven't been part of that life for a while now. I left and ventured off on my own. I find other caravans to travel with here and there, but things have changed, you know? Yes, I am sure you do. Anyway, I must still read your fortune, even if you do not want to share it with that man over there." Anslee leaned back from the table, as if the distance would emphasize all the no's she wanted to say.

The woman clamped her hands to the table, effectively trapping her in her place. "Oh no, don't fear it! You must let me, even if it's just as a favor for an old friend. Oh, and if your friend asks, call me Madame Mauve. Can't have the rabble knowing my real name, you know?" She winked.

And so Anslee found herself in a chair she had never wanted to sit in again. Why couldn't you just say no and walk off and be done with it? Now you have to sit through this frustrating nonsense. And worse, she had to bandy about this nonsense when Lord Varrock undoubtedly asked what she had learned. This seat brought back too many uncomfortable memories of her past, ones she had thought buried long ago. Memories that prevented her from moving forward in the new way of life she wanted.

Words cut through her internal chastisement.

"Is there a favorite method you have?" Cria asked.

Anslee's blank stare confirmed the answer.

"No, I thought not. You never were one for parting the veil between the hidden world and ours, were you? I know you hate the tarot cards most of all—too fickle, too unresponsive to the times. We shall use the ball then. Give your young man the show that he was hoping for."

Cria took the translucent glass ball and placed it between them at the table, then swiped her hands together and shook out her wrists. "I will forgo any of the so-called spells I usually have to start with. You would not be impressed with them anyway. Any wish you keep hidden will soon reveal itself to me."

Anslee couldn't tell if Cria was teasing or speaking seriously. She lowered her head over the crystal ball intently, and her bright blue eyes peered up at Anslee through the folds of her headscarf. She had to admit the overall effect was much more mysterious than she had originally expected, and she tensed. Would her future be empty nothingness again? She wiped her palms against her skirt, hoping Cria wouldn't notice her subtle movement.

Cria's brows furrowed. "My, my, now this is mysterious, love. Normally in a situation like this I'd see all sorts of trivial concerns—images of past infidelity, flashes of worry, feelings of anticipation... But with you? I do not see any of this. It's much murkier than normal." She rubbed her hand against the side of the ball, and Anslee noticed that the clear ball had filled up with a dark cloudy smoke. Cria hadn't been exaggerating. It brushed aside at the touch of Cria's hand, but as soon as she removed it, the smoke jumped back in place, obscuring what else might be hidden beneath the orb. She glanced at Anslee again, who stared back stoically. True, she was more invested in this than she had been earlier, but she also knew the roamers employed all sorts of tricks and sleight of hand to keep up their illusions and pretenses.

Cria grunted her annoyance, as if she knew Anslee didn't take her seriously. "Still do not believe in us, eh? You, of all people, should know that magic is real by now, Lee. It covers your past! I am getting... allusions to a warning, dark predators circling, and a sense of accomplishment when dark dreams become realized. These are all glimpses of things happening around you."

The smoke moved as if by its own violation, and a dark green tinge curled through the center, like a tiny bud unfolding. Cria eyed her through the lace and kept her hands pressed against the glass ball. Anslee noticed a small trickle of sweat sliding down the side of Cria's face, and leaned forward expectantly, as if she could help somehow.

"Do not touch me!" Cria's harsh whisper had her jumping back in her seat. "This is strong magic at play. It is awakening in the land, perhaps within you. But still, your future is..." Her eyes closed, and when they opened, the same murky darkness that was present in the orb crept through the blue of her eyes. Anslee jumped back, and sat down firmly on her hands. She could not place her finger on it, but she had a distinct feeling that she should not let Avery know this was not the innocent game of chance he had expected. Her shawl slipped down her back, and goosebumps prickled her skin. So far, this fortune was turning just as ominous as she had feared.

"Your future is just as dark as your past, Lee." Her eyes closed and opened again, this time fully black. Clouds shifted in her eyes as she addressed Anslee. "Who are you? I see nothing for you, about you, around you. It's almost as if you do not even have a future. But you do! There is not a time where it... ends, as I would see if death were in your future. It just ceases to exist. You cease to exist. It is a dark time for this kingdom, Lee, and somehow you are wrapped up in it."

Anslee couldn't ignore the darkness in the woman's eyes. "That's impossible. We are the strongest we've ever been after the return of our princess."

The black smoke left Cria's eyes in an instant, and her icy eyes stared back at Anslee. She slowly removed her hands from the orb and straightened from her hunched position. When she next spoke, her voice was harsh and haughty.

"Laugh if you will, Anslee. But something bad is brewing in you. Do not come back here. Do not search me or my people out. We want no part in the evil you are bringing to this kingdom," she hissed between clenched teeth. Cria's ferociousness startled Anslee. Cria was certainly taking this whole psychic reading much more seriously than she had expected. Almost as if she was a true believer. "Take your man and get out. Don't bring us the wolves hunting you."

Anslee stood slowly, following Cria's lead, and nodded briefly before turning on her heel and rushing off to Avery. Anslee had not wanted this reading anyway, and it left her creeped out. She remembered her nightmare from a few days ago. That creature with glowing red eyes and talons... Was this the one of the wolves Cria was referring to?

Anslee gave Avery an offhand remark about false prophecies, obsessions with trinkets, etc., and pulled him along down the path. She wanted him far away from Cria, where there was no chance of her past accidentally being brought up, or any of this misdirected anger to take hold. Unfortunately, Avery had other plans.

She swung Avery around when she brushed past him, tugging him back on the path towards the way they came.

Her blood boiled in her ears. Where did Cria get off telling her she brought death and destruction? Pretending to recognize her and be her friend, then demanding she leave. She stomped away, unable to hear Avery's words over her own pounding anger. It wasn't until she felt herself yanked backward, losing her footing and stumbling into Avery, that she realized he wasn't letting her lead him away.

"What was that, my dear?" He raised an eyebrow quizzically. "I paid good money for that wench to read your fortune, and I'd like to know what I bought."

She stammered. What to tell him? She was the harbinger of death? She knew that woman? Or brush it off and pretend she had been told of a future of getting married and having babes? Anxious tittering laughter peeled from her lips.

"Nothing of importance, my lord. I suspect that she, like all others in this park, prey upon those of lesser minds who are eager to believe her lies." She snapped the words out, daring him to contradict her. He frowned, turned back towards Cria, who was blatantly staring at them but quickly diverted herself with peering into her crystal ball. She truly believed what she had told him. She had always thought Cria's type of magic was a hoax, but would he believe her? He sighed and stepped up to join her.

"If she's as commonplace as you say she is, then let's be on our way. We'll run into another, and see if she has a better fortune to give you."

Anslee hid her scoff. He knew so little of the roamer ways. There wouldn't be another so-called fortune teller in this park, not today, at least. And even if there was, Anslee would rather admit to being a former roamer than allow that hoax to be played on her again.

16

I watch her from the woods. She never sees me. I am careful of that. But I see her. Gaily laughing and skipping along. Ignoring the omens that present themselves to her, the darkness that confronts her daily. I watch her encounter my own people, and while I want to rush out and strangle those that terrify her. I hold my place.

I once thought it would be I who would awaken her. I who would protect her and bring her joy every day of her life. But our paths diverged long ago, and I see that trail was never meant for me. It was laid out for another. I grumble and shift my feet, but don't move forward to intercept her. I thought about finding her once, long ago, but I never set out. I failed by refusing to try, and I will suffer for that.

17

Several weeks passed, and Avery continued to court her. He would take her for long walks, occasionally appear with horses to ride, or send small tokens of his affection. Anslee would wake up and perform her morning tasks with Magda, then rush upstairs and change, waiting for Avery to call on her. Some days he was late, some days, he did not appear, but most times, he was there promptly after lunch. He'd pick her up and take her to orchestra concerts, walks in the park, out for tea. She met no friends of his, but that only bothered her a little. Was he ashamed of her? After all, she did not have any friends to introduce him to either. He was always chaste, never inappropriate. She wondered if they really were only the friends he had insisted upon.

When she tried discussing this with Magda, she vehemently shut her down. "I've never had a friend send me such fantastic gifts," Magda had told her with raised eyebrows. When Anslee persisted, she threw down the towel she was using to wipe her hands. "If you are so certain that something is off, then why don't you just ask him? You spend almost every day with him. He sends you gifts nonstop. You do nothing else! Are you worried that you are just a little piece on the side, and he has a loving family at home you've never heard about? Preposterous. He's never even tried to kiss you or do anything more than politely take your hand. I've seen it, Anslee, and he is the perfect, controlled gentleman. Stop trying to rock the boat when there are no waves."

Cowed, Anslee finished her chores and slipped out of the kitchen in silence. Magda couldn't understand. She'd never had a family of her own. But Anslee had. And you didn't hide what you weren't ashamed of from your family.

He must not care for me like that, she told herself morosely.

One afternoon Avery picked her up, telling her he had a surprise.

"Oh?" she asked, wondering what he could possibly offer her that would not surprise her. Outings with him had turned into an endless round of surprises. "And what might that be?"

"If I told you, then it would not be a surprise, would it?" He winked and held out his hand, indicating she should step into his carriage that he drove on most visits. Once he helped her in, he quietly sat opposite her, staring out the window. Shadows enveloped them in the carriage. Her lord was not one for unnecessary small talk. It was a wonder he had ever introduced himself to her in the first place. He normally stared out the windows on their rides, watching those they passed and saving words for once they arrived at their destination. She wondered what he thought of this land he had emigrated to. She had considered his silence awkward at first, but had grown accustomed to using the time to study his features and discern his mood based on his facial expressions. In the light of day, nothing suspicious followed them. She wondered if she had imagined the awe of their earlier encounters.

He kept a tight control on his emotions and frowned often, his brow furrowed in thought. Whenever she asked him what bothered him, he waved his hand and gave an offhand comment about troubles with his work. She never pressed for a more permanent or indicative answer. Knowing he worked closely with the crown, she no longer asked, knowing she would not receive any answer of substance.

Instead, she let herself appreciate his gorgeous features and impeccable taste in clothes. Today he wore a deep red brocade tunic and jacket, with pin-striped brown and maroon pants. His favorite brown boots were polished to a shine—she had never seen him wear a scuffed pair of shoes. She shuffled her own feet to ensure they were in the middle of her skirt folds that fell to the floor. She did not own a single pair of shoes that weren't scuffed.

The carriage came to an abrupt stop, and Avery hopped up to open the door to murmur with the driver. Curious about the wait, Anslee stuck her head out the window, but Avery was there, blocking her view.

"Don't look. There's been an attack, and our route is being diverted," he said.

She pulled back, aghast. "An attack? What happened?"

His scowl darkened. "Wild animals, they think. It's the middle of the day, and the bodies are still here." He shook his head in disgust before swinging open the door to climb back inside. Anslee scooted back to allow him room, but not before she caught glimpses of the torn bodies behind him, blood splattered on the ground around them. She turned away, feeling sick. Was this what would have become of her if she hadn't escaped the shadow monster that attacked her a few weeks ago? She wrapped her arms around herself, but Avery remained indifferent, glaring out the window as if put out that these corpses had diverted their plans. He had never seemed so cold to her.

The carriage rumbled to a stop, and Anslee hopped up to open the door and escort her down. As Magda had earlier mentioned to her, always the perfect gentleman. She looked up and realized they stood outside a jewelry store. Her heart fluttered.

"What are we doing here?" She tried to keep her voice light, but her voice trembled slightly. He smiled at her, patting her arm.

"This is the surprise, my dear! I thought we could get something to update that old trinket you insist on wearing." He smiled at her, and he swept open the door for her.

Her hands reached up to unclasp the necklace that Robin had gifted her with. She supposed she did not need to wear it constantly. But she also wasn't sure that she wanted to remove the locket. It was the only reminder of a person she once considered home.

The proprietor of the shop came forward at the sound of tinkling bells. The woman's unexpected squeal caused Anslee to clamp her hands over her ears, forgetting about her sentimental thoughts.

"Lord Varrock! I am so glad you finally made it to the shop. We've had the item made just so to your specifications. I was unsure of the dimensions you required, but you have exquisite taste, my lord. I should not have been concerned. The—"

"Ahem," Avery raised his fingers to his pursed lips and pointed to Anslee. "A gift for my dear friend. I would prefer to hand it to her before you spout off all its features, if you do not mind."

The woman blushed, and her whole face lit up despite Avery's chastisement. She stepped to the side as she noticed Anslee for the first time. More likely, as she ran her eyes up and down over her person and her outfit, she had mistaken her as a servant, and now was getting a second look to see who she was dealing with. The woman dropped into a brief curtsy, saying she'd be back.

"Avery, this is too much. You really shouldn't have," Anslee protested, awkwardly backing up towards the door and waving her hands. Whatever he had envisioned, it was too much. Perhaps if she left, and disengaged from the moment... then they would not have to speak of it again. Small trinkets were one thing. But a piece of jewelry designed specifically for her... that spoke of a relationship far deeper than the one they had. A relationship she hadn't dared broach with him.

He walked toward her and put his hands on her shoulders, holding her in place. "Do not be so silly. You do not even know what it is."

She gestured around them. "I can imagine it's much too expensive, and you should not have done it."

He raised an eyebrow to challenge her. "You did not have a problem when I sent you the gown, and that was before I knew you." He raised his hand to her mouth to hush her protestations. Her whole body tensed as he lowered his mouth to her ear. "I know you so much better now, Anslee. Do you not think I deserve to show my adoration for you with a small gift?" He pulled his head away to look her in the eye, but his hands stayed firmly on her shoulders, rooting her in place. Little did he know, she would not have twitched a single muscle if he had moved them away, she was yearning so badly to hear what he had to say.

"You were my first friend when I came here, Anslee," he whispered, although no one else was in the room. Goosebumps rose on her arms. "The truth is, you've been my only friend since I've been here. I haven't wanted to meet anyone else. I haven't needed to. You," he lowered his head slightly. "You are all I've needed to survive here, although I did not know it when I arrived."

His eyes searched hers for answers she did not have. Questions she was not ready to answer. And then he pressed his lips to hers. She closed her eyes and relaxed into his hold, letting him grip her shoulders and kiss her harder.

Butterflies swirled in her stomach and tingled through her fingertips, which she placed against his broad chest. He tasted like forbidden fruit, the lord she thought she would never have, and her mind flashed wildly back to the pomegranate incident. He had appeared there, as if by magic, and now he was here, pressed against her. She leaned on her tiptoes to push her mouth against his, but his hands remained on her shoulders, rooting her back down. Perhaps she had been worried for nothing, and he wanted more out of their friendship. He was right here, asking for more. Warmth spread through her, and when he broke the kiss, she leaned forward, ready for more.

"Ahem."

The awkward noise had Anslee jerking her head backward, but Avery's grip on her remained firm, so she could only blush furiously. The shopkeeper was back, and had a much cooler disposition as she eyed the two of them together. She walked over and presented Avery with a small wooden box. It had an unfamiliar stamp on the front—she assumed it was the crest of the Varrock estate, although she had never seen it before. Otherwise, the box was simple and unadorned. With his back to her, he peeked inside the box. Confirming everything was as expected, and turned back to face her, the shop girl hovering beyond his shoulder.

"My dear, it has been a whirlwind moving here and learning all the city has to offer. I must admit, that if not for your particular friendship, I would have grown homesick long, long ago. I thought it only fitting to gift you with a reminder of my home." He flicked open the case to reveal a simple chain with an elaborate red gem on the end of the necklace. Her mind flashed to the promise necklace those girls at the market had spoken of weeks ago. Was this a sort of declaration?

He watched her face as she tentatively reached out a hand and ran it down the side of the necklace and lifted the jewel to see it better. Did he know the lore of the promise necklace? Was that why he gave this to her?

"Is this a ruby?" she asked, choking out the last word. She had never seen such a large stone, much less owned one. Upon closer inspection, she realized it wasn't one large stone, but a medium-sized stone with smaller stones, precisely cut and placed in a teardrop around the larger one.

Noticing her gaze, he explained, "It is much harder to take the smaller stones and find ones of equal size and quality. And once equal stones are mined, to place them all around the larger one mimicking how these are naturally found—it's then extra work to separate them and fix them together in a way that's much less likely to break. That's why this is often called the 'flower stone.'" He hesitated, as if stopping himself from saying more.

She looked up questioningly. Would this be one of those times he rebuffed her questions? "What else are they called?"

Avery looked pained at the question and averted his eyes. "Commonly, people referred to these as blood stones in my land," he mumbled.

"That seems rather morbid." And not at all in line with the kiss they had just shared.

"You've never heard that term before?" He looked at her quizzically. "I suppose I shouldn't be so surprised. Perhaps you've never seen a blood stone before either?" She shook her head, still caressing the necklace in its box. He noted her movement and smiled. "I am glad you like it, at least. Here, let me put it on you." She lifted her hair and unclasped the locket she was wearing. Not knowing what to do with it, she held it awkwardly in her hand. Stepping behind her to clasp the necklace around her throat, he continued. "These are found naturally on the edge of the eastern side of the kingdom, right near where I live, in fact. It's rumored that out past the kingdom's borders into the wild is an endless supply of these flower-shaped gems. They aren't quite rubies—they harden into larger shapes incredibly quickly compared to your normal gem, which also makes them very fragile. The slightest movement in the stone that houses them and the gem fractures, forming a very similar flower pattern to the one now around your neck."

He ran his hand down the necklace till he cupped the jewel at the end, right against her breast. She gave a sharp intake of breath at the memory of their interrupted kiss. Would he again?

"This looks lovely with your coloring. A perfect match." His hand dropped away, and he took a step back, turning to speak with the shopkeeper to finalize payment.

He turned back to her after a few last pleasantries with the shopkeeper. "Now, how about we leave that locket you were wearing here? You will not be needing it anymore, now that you have a new one to wear every day."

She jerked her hand away as he reached for it. "This one is just a trinket. I can put it away back in the manor."

"We will leave it here. You will not need to wear it again. It's a dull, tawdry thing." Avery's fingers tried to coax the locket loose, and in their fumbling, it flew out of her hand and skidded a few feet across the floor.

"Oh! Let me get that for you, Lord Varrock." And the shopkeeper was racing over and picking up the locket. Anslee assumed she would do anything to help poor Lord Varrock, who was stuck here with such a simpleton she did not even realize the worth of the present she was being given.

The woman's movements slowed as she picked up the locket. Anslee knew it was a simple silver locket in a plain heart shape. The only unique feature was the tiny swirls of gold around the edges. Nothing to catch the attention of the woman who worked with more elaborate jewelry. The shopkeeper snapped open the inside of the locket, as if curious what she would find, but the inside was lacking, devoid of any pictures or mementos. She looked up at Avery's glaring face. His next words were icy to her.

"I believe that locket belongs to my companion. Neither of us gave you leave to toy with it," Avery said coldly. Anslee stared at him. He hadn't cared about it before. In fact, he had been eager to be rid of it. An icy breeze swept through the room, ruffling his hair, but the door never opened.

The shopkeeper gripped it in her hand, ignoring the sudden cold. "Lord Avery, this locket resembles one of several items that were stolen from our shop a few weeks ago. It's what kept us from completing your order so quickly. I find it odd, to say the least, that this woman enters wearing an exact copy of one of our designs." Anslee froze. Being accused of stealing, like a common thief, like a *roamer*, hit too close to home for her. She hadn't stolen it. But what if Robin had?

Avery sneered at her. "Not a unique design to worry so much about it. We can easily clear this up, I am sure. Anslee, where did this locket come from? I assume it was some remembrance of your past since you are always wearing it," he rolled his eyes to look at her, relaxed in his stance. He almost seemed bored by the exchange. The sudden chill settled, then warmed. Unless that was the blush creeping across her cheeks as she thought of Robin.

"It came from a friend. From a long time ago." Knowing her words were misleading, they still slipped out of her mouth. She clutched her hands tightly, trying not to rush forward and snatch her locket out of that woman's hands. How dare she think she could take her things? And accuse her of stealing. Although, she felt the inklings of doubt trickle through her. Robin had thrown her that locket. Robin, who she had grown up with among half-truth tellers and roamers who did not think it at all averse to pick up something they fancied without paying for it. She pushed those thoughts aside. Robin had never been like that. He had always had the good conscience and moral heart that her people had lacked. But he had been running away when he gave it to her... Who was to say he hadn't been running from this very shop with a whole handful of treasure?

"See? All settled." Avery reached out his hand expectantly, and the shopkeeper dropped the locket into it. It seemed he had forgotten his desire to leave the locket here. He once more touched the blood stone locket already placed around Anslee's neck, but it felt like a chain anchoring her in place, preventing her from going after the shopkeeper.

"Shall we?" He turned, presenting his arm to Anslee and slipping her locket in his pocket. She took his hand and let him escort her back out to the carriage, waiting until they were alone before demanding he return her locket to her. He settled into his side of the carriage, not even noticing her irritated stare at him.

"Avery? Can I have my locket back now?"

He shifted his gaze from the windows back to her. Her dark eyes pierced her, staring into her soul. Gone was the tender, emotional man who had whispered in her ear and gifted her with this necklace. He stared at her with the gaze of a predator. "And why would you want that?"

She shook her head, clearing the comparison of him and a hungry wolf from her mind. "It's an emotional gift for me, Avery. It reminds me of my childhood." Why was he so insistent that she give it up? Her mind turned dark. Was he trying to brand her? Claim her as his, perhaps?

"And now this necklace will remind you of adulthood. Of me." He cocked his head quizzically, as if trying to figure her out.

"Of course, this necklace will!" She gripped the locket she now wore about her neck. She appreciated the sentiment, of course, but right now she wanted to rip it off and throw it at his feet. One gift didn't give him leave to reduce her past to nothing. She didn't need to be claimed. Her fingers paled from how tightly they clenched around the locket.

"But that doesn't mean I just throw away every other gift I've ever received. Should I trash the lovely gown you gifted me with when we first met since now you've given me a new necklace? No, of course not. Well, this is the same thing. So, please, Avery." She held out her hand, imploring him to drop the locket in her palm. It hadn't been a promise chain from Robin. She knew that. But still... he had been her closest childhood friend. They had grown up together, and giving away something he gave her felt like cutting off a part of herself.

Avery conceded, and rubbed his eyes and pushed his hair back with his hands. "That is sound logic I had not expected." She ignored the subtle dig at her intelligence. He smiled, and she wondered how she could ever have compared him to a predator. Perhaps the slight had been unintended.

"You do things differently here in the capital than the ways I am used to. I apologize for angering you, Anslee." He settled back in his seat, and she smiled tentatively, not sure what to say to him to make this alright. He reached out to grab her fingers in his hand, and her heart warmed at this new contact. Unnoticed darkness dripped beneath her fingers, pooling on the carriage floor before rolling away, unnoticed by even Avery.

It was only right that she wear a tangible token of his affection to show she was under his protection. But who did she need to be protected from? Her mind whirled with thoughts of shadow predators, magic, missing crowns, and bounties until they arrived in front of the manor. She left him now wearing a small fortune around her neck, and the old locket clutched in her hand.

18

The dark stone path glinted in the setting sun as she hurried down it. Magda had insisted she travel to her favorite baker to get cheese. She shook her head in annoyance. In reality, Magda had just wanted to get her out of the house for a while. Probably hoping for some stolen time with the butcher. It was obvious.

She pulled her cloak tighter about her and hurried down the road. Her destination was out on the edge of town, so it had seemed like a nice walk with the sun shining when she left. Summer had passed surprisingly quickly this year. Normally, she reveled in the long summer nights and humid air that blew across the land. She was quick to partake in the spontaneous dances that originated in the capital's Circle, but those had also been few this year. Ironic, since with the return of the missing princess, the King and Queen had hosted balls for themselves and foreign dignitaries. The townsfolk had not been invited to join any more of the merry-making, and the good cheer had slowly stopped trickling down to the masses. Now, the cold air was blowing, and the people were preparing for a chilly winter.

She hurried, trying to beat the encroaching darkness. Ever since being attacked by that shadow creature, she had avoided the nighttime when possible. It had once felt like peace and beauty to her, but now every shadow brought the fear that something vicious could jump out and snap at her. She wrapped her cape tighter around herself as if it could protect her from her thoughts.

The only good thing about the cold blowing in was this new cape Avery had gifted her with. It was bright scarlet, flowing, and she adored throwing it on and traipsing about town. Unfortunately, there was no one out and about this far outside of town to admire how dignified she looked. But that did not stop her from enjoying the pretty coat for herself. She knew as soon as the biting winter came, she'd have to resort to her old dusty standby. It felt made of tough rawhide (looked that way too), but no biting wind or snowy cold ever blew through the sturdy fabric.

Even though fall had come early this year, she decided to enjoy it. Life was going so well otherwise. Things with Magda were more or less the same, the dreary lord she worked for had gotten a little sick in this year's cold, but that just meant less work for her to do around the house, even compared to her normal limited chores. Avery was attentive and charming, as usual. She worried about what would happen when he returned back to his estates to tend things at home, but he often assured her that with the princess returning, he had too many duties at the castle to warrant leaving. She still did not quite understand what he did during the day, but he kept her occupied with tales of his homeland and questions about life in the Capital, and she never quite thought to ask him about his other daily obligations when they were together.

The sound of crunching leaves had her pause a moment. A few leaves straggled across her path, but this sounded like the crunching of forest leaves piled high underfoot. Oh goddess, was that another shadow beast? Or just the wind picking up pace with her? Anslee drew her hood closer and chanced a glance back behind her. There was nothing. No bright eyes glared at her from the lengthening shadows. She had felt trapped within the streets of the town, walled in by tall buildings. But now she realized those had been protection against the elements. Out here, in the woods bordering the town, she was alone and vulnerable, with no one to come when she called for help.

She was being paranoid. She lowered her head to hurry along more quickly. Perhaps if she could make it there and return before it was completely dark tonight. She was too conspicuous on the edge of town with her bright cherry colored cloak. An easy target for anyone —anything—out hunting her. Was that a scuffling of paws? She paused and raised her head, taking a moment to double check the noises she was hearing.

An arrow whisked by her arm, and she jumped right before a body slammed into her, pushing her to the ground. Panic flooded through her as someone locked her arms against the ground. Her hood flopped over her face, and she wasn't able to see who was attacking her. Her cape aided her captor in keeping her down and confused. She struggled against the person on top of her, trying to jerk her head free and kicking out with her legs. She heard a decidedly male groan as she struck home at his most sensitive spot. She took the brief relapse to slide partially out from under him. He reached to drag her toward him, and the two tumbled off the side of the road and into the low ditch alongside it.

Her hood rolled off during the tackle, and she looked up into the panting face of Robin. He stared at her, hazel eyes opening wide before quickly sliding off her.

"Oh, Lee," he breathed out. "I am so, so sorry. Are you hurt?" He reached out to slide his hand along her arm, but she kicked out at him with her feet, now tangled in her cloak, and scooted back against the dirt and fallen leaves.

"Get away from me! Don't touch me!" she snarled.

"I'm sorry! It was a misunderstanding. Don't you see?" He kept his distance, holding out his hands to show he was weaponless

"No, I do *not* see! How could I possibly think that was an accident!" She snarled back at him, body tense and preparing to run if he made another move against her. This was her Robin? How could this be her Robin!

"You're injured. Let me help you." He glanced at her arm and back to her face, and she noticed for the first time blood oozing out of a long, sharp cut in her arm. Apparently, that arrow had not completely passed her like she thought it had. Adrenaline surged through her, keeping the pain at bay and her words sharp.

"I am sure it would be fine if you hadn't ground it in the dirt as you tackled me," she growled, observing the cut through the torn fabric. It was much deeper than she first thought, and she was sure she would need stitches for the wound to heal back up. Anslee grimaced in pain as the adrenaline wore off and the pain from her cut spread throughout her arm. She shifted her weight, trying to free her feet for a getaway. She gasped as it twisted her arm the wrong way. Quickly, she rolled and placed all her weight on her other arm.

"Lee, really, you need help with that. I am terribly sorry about this. But you have to let me help you. I could have done some real damage to you!" His face warred between the anguish at causing her pain and the determination to let him help her. He had given her similar looks as a young child—a look of worry, concern, and stubbornness that she had been all too familiar with given her reckless, high-handed ways. How had they gotten to this point?

"I will go nowhere with you. Tell me why you attacked me. Tell me why you thought I was a threat!" She leaned back on her one good elbow, dizziness from blood loss taking its effect.

His face crumpled, but his hand remained outstretched to help her in case she fell over completely. "I would never hurt you, Lee."

"Well, you did," she snapped, trying to keep her tone ferocious despite the pain.

He winced again. "But it wasn't on purpose! With that cloak, and that... jewel at your neck, we thought you were one of... just someone with money. And many people need all the help they can get right now. We never meant to hurt you. Just take some of the wealth you were bandying about with." His gaze lingered on the blood stone that Avery had given her. She wore it every day, replacing the locket she had worn for a few short weeks. On days she did not wear it, Avery asked about it, concerned that somehow outgrowing his gift would mean the same as outgrowing him. So she always wore it, just so he would not ask.

"Please, Lee. At least let me see that your arm gets taken care of, and then I can get you home safely. There will be nothing else to worry about the rest of the night, and you will not have to see me again after that." When she did not answer, he moved to help her up with her good arm, and she staggered against him, the blood loss hitting her as she tried to stand on her own two feet.

"What gives you the right to decide who is worthy of their possessions and who is not?" she grunted, struggling to keep pace. He glanced at her sidelong, then went back to scouting the area ahead of them. No doubt looking for his companions in their attempted robbing. At his sharp whistle and raised hand motion, she shook her head in disgust.

"The same right that gives my people the chance at survival," he muttered. "But you would know nothing about that, would you, Anslee?" His gaze darkened as he took in her town cloak and blood stone necklace again. "You seem to enjoy a noble existence these days. You used to be one of us."

Her heart cracked as he used her formal name instead of the nickname he had always called her.

But his flippant tone also angered her. "How could you pretend to know anything about me, Robin? You haven't seen me in years, and then you only come when you want something," she said. She tried to keep the hurt out of her accusatory tone, and she looked away so he would not see it in her eyes either.

"I've had people keeping an eye on you. You didn't seem like you needed me then or now." His words were distant, as if he was trying hard to keep a rein on his roiling emotions. He kept a firm grip around her waist as he led her further into the forest, now sprawling them on either side of the road. She leaned away from him as much as possible. Despite needing his help to walk, she detested his touch. She hoped she wasn't walking into a trap, but at this point she had little choice. What would she do by herself on the side of the road?

"Besides, you live in that fancy town manor," Robin continued angrily, "with your new *boyfriend* keeping you company. Do you even have the necklace I gave you? Or did you throw it out like your past?"

Her foot caught on a sharp divot in the ground, buried by the fallen leaves, and the quick pain from jostling her arm made her gasp.

Stopping, Robin settled her down and turned her arm in his hands with practiced motions. "Shit, this is deeper than I thought. We need to bind it." He placed her arms down and pulled a plain knife from his boot tops. He reached into the sack he carried around his back and pulled out a roll of bandages, stripping a section off. "I've learned a few things since our days tumbling around," he told her ruefully. He picked off the twigs and leaves that were stuck in the coagulating blood before wrapping up her arm. She winced at the pressure and every movement that tugged at her skin, but kept still.

His worried eyes met hers, "I am sorry this hurts. But you know it's necessary."

His hands were smooth and methodical as he went through the practiced motions. She tried not to think of his hands tending his wounds, and how this reminded her of a thousand other small cuts and bruises he had tended to.

"Obviously," she snapped, pushing him away. "Just as walking away with you after you tried to rob me is necessary to fix the injury that you caused."

The tenderness that had been filling his eyes immediately fled, and the emotions showing in his face shut down at her tone. "Then let's hurry and get you fixed," he said. "So I can return you to your lover and your fancy manor in the capital."

"Stop pretending like you know anything about me, Robin. Some stupid jewelry doesn't entitle you to anything." She was fuming, the heat rushing to her cheeks. She just wished he would take a swing at her, so she could throw her own punches and get all this anger out of her chest. So what if once he had been her sun and stars, and she thought the world revolved around him? So what if he had made her worries fade away? Being with him now made breathing difficult.

"I know enough," he muttered darkly. They walked the rest of the way in silence, twilight quickly filtering through all the surrounding trees. She would not be making it home early tonight.

Eventually, she heard the noises of the roamer camp, a lifestyle she had left long ago. When two sentries stepped behind some trees to halt them, they saw Robin and his captive. With the wave of his hand, they passed through without stopping. Long gone were the days when the two of them had scampered off and hidden away from the scouts set up around the perimeters to protect them. She glanced at Robin. The sentries hadn't even questioned him. When she lived here, the only person to never be questioned was their pack leader... Roamers protected their own, and part of that over protectiveness and stubbornness meant strictly enforced borders. Only roamers in or out. And they always needed a reason. Except for Robin apparently... Maybe things had changed.

A few steps later they walked into one of the makeshift roamer villages she had grown up among. Kids scampered between tents with slow burning fires outside of them, and laundry strung up against the tree branches, slowly drying between the heat of the fire and the cool, blowing wind. People went about their daily lives, mostly ignoring them. Some nodded at Robin if they glanced in his direction, with only a few quizzical glances thrown at her. So far, she did not recognize any of the people around her. He led them between several tents before arriving at the medical healer's abode. A group of roamers sat around a fire, gossiping about the town.

"And then the magic lapped against the sides of the palace!""Turned the crowd into a mob, I hear," said a burly man sitting around the fire.

A red-headed woman slapped him upside the head. "Don't be daft, Bern. I was there. A lot of drunk shenanigans but no threat of a real mob."

Bern's eyes narrowed. "And what about this business of a crown? Aye, that money could do us good."

"Help us buy some extra weapons! Protect against the things that howl *awoooo* in the night!" A series of cheers went up, and Anslee shivered.

"As if we need whatever ill fortune that damned crown would bring about. With magic up in the air like this again, no good can come of something that's been missing," the red-haired woman continued. She had to be the force of reason here. It was eerie how similar her reasoning was to Anslee's. She tried to hear what else they said, but Robin led them inside the tent, storm clouds on his face.

She recognized the sign of a simple sprig leaf emblazoned on a creaking piece of wood hanging outside the door. She sniffed at the sharp, aromatic smell of burning herbs coming from the hut. Much different than the minty smell of the apothecary she had become accustomed to. Last time she had been in one of these healer's huts, she needed a deep wound on her leg stitched up. She had the scar to prove it. Robin had been right beside her then, holding her hand. She wrinkled her nose at the thought.

"Are our ways not good enough for you now?" Robin muttered under his breath. "At least try to keep your disgust to yourself while we put you back together. You can go back to your condescension once you leave." She didn't bother to correct him. The sooner she could be healed, the sooner she could leave and end their association... and all the uncomfortable feelings being here triggered.

The tent flap flung open, and an old man stooped with age stepped through the door. "Ah, Robin, what have you brought for me to mend this day? A rich little lady, by the looks of her." He eyes her cloak with open distrust, but Robin just smiled and reached out his hand for a quick shake.

"A case of mistaken identity on the road, nothing more. She got a little beat up in the scuffle, so if we can just fix her up, then she'll be on her way. Her arm needs tending." He reached around to pull forward the injured arm she had been cradling against her body. Despite his gentle hands, she hissed in pain, gritting her teeth. "I think she just needs some stitches, and then she'll be ready. I'll leave her in your capable hands and then be back to collect her later."

He avoided looking her in the eye as he gave his directions and walked away. She and the doctor eyed one another. She wondered if he'd been able to see well enough with his rheumy eyesight to even heal her, or if she'd end up with crooked stitches in her arm. Mutely, he indicated she enter his sacred workspace. She stepped through the tent flap into darkness. She had never planned on returning to a roamer camp. The cruelty of the sheriff that ultimately hunted down her father had dashed her few pleasant memories. No one here had protected him. She thought she had turned her back on these people for good, but here she was at their mercy.

19

The only light came from a slowly burning fireplace in the center of the tent. The only warmth too. It took a minute for her eyes to adjust. Despite the darkening sky outside the tent, she had at least been able to see around them from the rising moon and stars and the little sunlight that was left in the day. In here, the tent flaps effectively shut out all outside noise and light. She wondered if they set all tents up this way or just the healer's. Not that it mattered. As she followed the healer into the tent, she fingered the scratchy material of a wall. With a start, she realized it was the same material that made up her old winter coat. Not pretty to look at, but highly effective against the elements.

"These walls not up to your liking, lady? These structures serve our needs though, and they will suffice just fine while we fix that arm." His tone of voice was not apologetic, and she knew he was judging her for her fine clothes. She pursed her lips and withheld any comments.

He directed her to the stool below a narrow table littered with dried herbs and anesthesias. He took a seat beside her and slowly began unwrapping the bandage wrapped around her injury. Robin had bound her wound in haste, and a few leaves clung to the outside. Her cloak was still on, and the ripped strands were stuck in the wrapping. The old man tsk-ed as he unrolled the bandage. "Who bandaged this?" he asked her.

"Robin," she answered softly. He glanced up at her sharply, and she realized his eyes weren't rheumy at all. Just a clear, pale blue. It was as if all the color had been sucked out of them with age. Perhaps she would not leave here with uneven stitches. A coughing fit wracked his body, and his hands shook against her arm, rubbing the bandage painfully against her arm. She drew her arm back slightly.

"Perhaps I should find Robin, after all. It was silly to come all the way here. I am sure I can get help at home."

He glared at her and straightened her arm back out, fingers firm but gentle. "Afraid I'll be cutting into you with my old age and shaky hands?" he asked tartly. He went back to unwrapping her bandage until he revealed the entire bloody mess. "You need not worry. I have an apprentice to do the needlework. I am cleaning the wound so it's ready when she gets back." She relaxed a little at his words. Small favors to be thankful for, indeed.

He took the bloody bandages and dumped them in the trash on the other side of the tent before returning to wash his hands and clean out her cut with antiseptic. It burned, but she kept her mouth pressed tight and looked away, tears springing to her eyes at the stinging sensation. Thankfully, the old man continued to work in quiet, without trying to engage her in conversation. He looked almost peaceful, cleaning the wound, concentrating deeply on his work.

Eventually, he just had her take her cloak off once he was convinced there weren't any additional threads stuck in the cut that would cause more damage when she went to remove it. She still had to maneuver her arm out of the cloak, though, and that definitely hurt. He murmured soothing words of sympathy in encouragement, and she thought maybe he wasn't all bad for an old man.

"Grandfather! I'm back! Robin told me there was someone in here that would need stitches. Did not say who, though." Anslee's head jerked up at the sound of a young woman's voice soaring through the tent as she walked in backward, pulling a large tray of what must be their medical kit. She recognized that voice, and she jolted to the side, spilling the bottle of antiseptic.

"Argh!" The man lurched to save the antiseptic, but the glass bottle fell to the floor and crashed. The young woman whirled around and glared at Anslee.

"You!" Cria cried out. She helped her grandfather up, steadying him from falling over. "What are you doing here? I told you to stay away from me!"

"I did not bring myself here for the fun of it. I did not even bring myself here at all! Robin brought me after shooting me with a damn arrow!"

For once, Cria was silent. Even her grandfather looked surprised at this revelation. She remembered Robin hadn't specified how she had gotten injured and why she had needed to be brought back to this camp to be healed. She sniffed and looked away. Apparently he hadn't told Cria either. "It would have been nice for him to give you a head's up, seeing as how we all grew up together," she told Cria, offering a neutral statement as a peace offering.

"Oh no, don't turn this around on him. You should have never been over here in the first place. It's probably your own damn fault you're sitting in this chair."

Anslee opened her mouth to protest, then shut it like a gaping fish. Cria was already determined not to believe her, nor even to like her. Why should she even bother trying to explain the truth? Cria bent over to clear up the glass shards from the bottle Anslee had broken. When Anslee moved to get off the stool and help, Cria held up a hand.

"Don't. Just don't. We don't need you getting in the way any more than you already have. Stay put, and I'll deal with you after I clean up your mess."

Anslee pouted at the way Cria declared she'd 'deal' with her—as if she were just another mess dropped on her doorstep to clean up. She sighed. She supposed she was. Robin had dropped her here for just that reason, even if neither of them wanted to admit it. Why had he even brought her here if he was just going to abandon her? She sat quietly while Cria stitched her up and bound her wounds. No one in the tent said anything until Cria finished and left. Anslee wasn't part of this world anymore. Why had she let Robin bring her here to force more work on his people? She belonged at the manor with Magda or with Lord Varrock. She wrapped her bandaged arm around herself.

Sitting out here, surrounded by roamers, she had never felt more unworthy of the lord.

20

The old man slowly made his way back to his worktable, pouring two glasses of dark amber liquid before walking over with the two cups in hand. His eyes were as clear as ever.

"She's a firecracker, my granddaughter," he said with a chuckle. "Did not even offer you the bite of a drink to ease the pain of that sharp needle. But then again, you really got under her skin mentioning your encounter with Robin... and apparently the fact that she had recently seen you." He clinked his glass against hers. "Drink up, girl. No doubt you need it after that."

She brought the glass up to her nose and sniffed. Whiskey. But what else had she expected?

"Am I to toast with a stranger?" she asked him.

"Crio. It's a family name," he said, chuckling in response to her raised eyebrows. It was uncommonly similar to his granddaughter's name.

He lifted his glass again, nodding towards her full cup.

Anslee couldn't delay any longer without looking like a wimp, and giving further indication that she didn't belong here. She straightened her spine and took a swig of the stuff. Grinning, Crio followed her lead. It burned like fire going down, but she'd be damned if she gagged in front of him. Robin should be back soon, and then he'd be able to escort her home.

"Ah, that's better, isn't it? Now, I do not want to hear about whatever my granddaughter was going on about. She has her own reasons for doing things. I have mine. We'll drop you off with Robin. I assume you've been here long enough for whatever else he was taking care of."

Taking care of? Had dropping her off in here been a distraction for him? "Do not give me that questioning look. Robin's a busy man. I am sure he had several things to take care of that did not relate to you. Now, ah, my dear... Just through that entrance." He held open the tent flap and stepped back, waiting for her to step through. Who did these people think she was?

Something was obviously off because they seemed to have no idea she was just a servant in the city. A lousy, carefree servant, but still—not a free roamer. Cria, at least, knew she was not from this world anymore. And judging by her cloak and necklace, the others would have guessed as well. She was ready to get back to where she belonged. She followed the old man through the maze of tents on the way to their destination.

"That's an interesting necklace you have there, girl."

She put her hand up to her neck. This was the second time tonight someone had mentioned her necklace. Was it so rare for a roamer to see jewels? She laughed at the thought. Hah, of course not. She should know. She had lived it. Rare to wear jewels themselves, maybe, not when they were stolen.

"It was a gift from a friend," Anslee said.

"Oh, really now? Do you know the value of a gemstone? Especially one shaped like that?" Crio asked her.

"I know that they're valuable and naturally occurring," Anslee told him.

"Oh, ho ho," he laughed loudly but stopped when it turned into wheezing and a coughing spasm, bending over. He spat out whatever had been caught in his mouth. "Rarely naturally occurring. So rare that I could count on one hand how many times I've seen that shape." Avery had mentioned something of the sort, but it surprised Anslee to hear that an out-of-the-way roamer would know that as well.

"I hadn't realized it was so rare. Are you sure?" She was only half-listening. Her arm hurt. Her childhood friend had shot her, and then another had yelled and abandoned her. She wanted to be home in bed, not arguing with some old man.

"Oh, I am sure. One, on the crown of our very own dear King and Queen. The crown that's been missing these twenty years past," Crio said.

Anslee paused. Could it be a coincidence that bloodstones were on her necklace and had been part of the missing crown? She had tried so hard to suppress those memories. Had there truly been bloodstones on the crown? She had assumed those were rubies encircling it...

"But the missing princess..." she protested.

"I'll be damned if her sudden appearance without it bodes well for our country. Missing princess, my arse. What those monarchs really want is that crown." He shook his head. "Second, on the chests of warriors that live past the eastern wastelands. What? You thought the wastelands were actually bare?" He looked at her incredulously.

"And the third?" she asked anxiously, prodding him along. She expected the answer but couldn't stop herself from asking the question.

He raised his head and pointed at her necklace, all mirth gone from his face. "Right around your neck. And you show up just as things are getting interesting," he muttered.

"Getting interesting, how?" she asked softly. Her hand cradled her necklace. Crio had mentioned warriors from the eastern wastelands. Avery was from those eastern lands, but he had never mentioned warriors before. She was wondering if he was purposely leaving things out of his story and how he came to be in the capital.

But her question to Crio was lost in the hearty hale of Robin, hurrying toward them. The old man leaned over. "If I were you, girl, I would not wear that necklace so freely as you do. You're not only asking to be robbed by someone like him, you're also declaring an allegiance you know nothing about."

Then Robin was upon them, thanking the old man and seizing Anslee's arm to ensure the stitches looked clean and even. He nodded, thanked the man again, and turned off with Anslee in tow. She tried to pull back and ask the old man a final question. Who are you? What are you talking about? Allegiance to whom? How did this all connect to a mysterious lord named Avery Varrock, who hailed from the east? But she couldn't ask him that question. And Crio was avoiding eye contact now that Robin had arrived, and neither seemed inclined to let her do as she wished.

The old man had vanished when she turned back around, and she stopped walking. Robin, still gripping her arm, tugged her to a stop. "And what will you do with me now? Am I done being shuffled about from place to place? I believe you told me you'd see that I was properly taken care of and then returned home."

He turned to her, his eyes hard. "And do you not think you are being taken proper care of?"

She pulled her arm free and planted her feet, refusing to go forward. "I would like to go home."

"Gods, Lee! You were always stubborn." His voice was irritated and frustrated. "I sent a note to your home. There was no way I was letting you return home like this, especially not after what happened, and without the chance to explain myself. You'll be safe here for the night, and I can return you in the morning."

She bit her lip, contemplating her options. She was supposed to rise early to work with Magda tomorrow. Would she be home in time for that? Doubtful. No one here seemed to realize she was just a servant without control over her day to day activities. And what had they even told Magda? Had she believed them? Oh, gods above, what if she was out looking for her right now?

Robin must have seen the panic flashing through her eyes since he placed his hands on her shoulders, careful not to touch her injured arm too much. "Anslee, do you trust me? It's been taken care of, I promise." His face hardened. "And there are creatures out there that make it unsafe to travel in the dark. Come now, get some rest, and stay here where it's safe. I can't ensure your safety or that of my people if you try to leave."

So it came down to this. Did she trust Robin or the unknown more? She wavered, but the woods behind him did not look at all enticing. How had she run unabashedly through the forest as a child? But then, she had grown up in the Mistwood Forests, not the King's Wood, where Robin now hid his roamers. Surely, they couldn't look down on her for her fear of trespassing in these woods.

She reluctantly nodded her head. As children, he had always quieted her worries and fears. It seemed he still had that effect on her. Sighing, she let Robin lead her away to a temporary bedroll for the night, where she could wonder about the mystery of Avery and the bloodstones in peace.

21

The next morning dawned bright and early. She rolled to her shoulder, sitting up and blinking at the low sunlight filtering around her. Why did her bed feel harder than usual? She opened her eyes wider and blinked against the bright light streaming through the tent flaps. Suddenly she was wide awake. How had she forgotten she had stayed the night at Robin's campsite? She had to leave and return home.

She quickly jumped up and pulled on her coat, her wounded arm and stitches nearly forgotten. Birds chirped and trilled outside her tent as if hurrying her onward... or chastising her for still being here. She was running out the door to get home, not thinking about how she would even find her way when she ran into Robin holding a plate of food.

"In a hurry to leave? I take it you slept well." She had fallen asleep, listening to the crackling fireplace and cheerful chatter between friends happening outside her tent. He looked as if he had already been awake for hours.

"Yes, thank you," she said, remembering her manners.

"I was coming to see if you would break your fast with me. We had little time to talk last night, and as I am sure you know, I am terribly sorry about the misunderstanding and would love to make it up to you." He smiled and offered her the plate of cooked meats and bread. It smelled divine, but staying for a meal would indicate that she was willing to pick up their friendship. And she was not.

"That is very kind, Robin. But really, I must be leaving now. If you recall, I preferred to leave last night. Now, if you could be so kind as to show me my way back yourself or find someone who can..." She gestured at the surrounding village that was slowly waking up and beginning to bustle with activity.

He paused a moment, watching her survey the land. "Yes, of course," he finally said quietly. "Are you ready now, then? I can make sure you get back okay." She took a moment to take her bearings, making sure she did indeed have everything she had come here with. She fingered her necklace, the cause of so much trouble, reassuring herself that it still was around her neck before nodding. "If you won't sit with me, then at least eat on your way back. You must be starving." He handed her the food as they set out. As long as he knew she wasn't staying, Anslee told herself guiltily. She shoved a roll into her mouth. She had been starving.

"I had an interesting talk with that old man last night," she said around a mouthful of bread.

"Crio? He doesn't normally talk to other people. Strange that he opened up with you."

"He seemed to have some opinions that I have not heard before."

"Like what?" He eyed her warily, although he still spoke in a friendly, open tone. She toyed with her expensive necklace but said nothing else. She did not want to bring up the topic if he would not initiate it.

"It doesn't matter. Why don't you tell me what you've been doing that caused you to shoot at me?"

He winced as if he was the one shot with an arrow. Robin had always insisted that he would not steal for his own profit. It had been a very unpopular opinion when they were growing up together, although he had mostly kept it to himself. Still, gossip like that traveled fast. Most people had assumed Robin had a holier-than-thou attitude and ignored him. Perhaps that was why they had had few childhood friends growing up.

"Well, Robin? What do you have to say for yourself? Have you given up all your great and lofty ideals to become nothing more than a petty thief?" He had once told her how the roamers should give up their thieving ways and live off the land, like proper farmers, or rely on their entertainment methods for profit. Looking back on it now, it seemed incredibly naïve.

His eyes flashed with anger. He opened his mouth to retort but only gaped at her. She saw him visibly compose himself, and some veins she had not noticed before were popping out on his forehead. Where had his sudden anger come from?

"What have you heard about the land in the last few months?"

Her blank stare said it all.

"That is what I thought." He grimaced. "I am sure you've been *busy* these past few months, and perhaps news of the change has not reached city dwellings yet." He emphasized busy, no doubt mocking her budding romance. "But I am telling you, Lee, bad things are happening." With the cheery bustling of the camp they walked through, the trilling birds, and the hearty smells of breakfast, she couldn't believe him.

"What things?" She thought uneasily of Magda telling her the lord was considering closing up the town manor and retiring to the countryside. What had once seemed a frivolous plan to secure her future had turned into a necessity weighing on her mind. Surely, Robin couldn't know about that.

"It's hard to explain. But the woods... they are not safe anymore. At least, not like they used to be."

She jumped at the loud clanging of a woman setting up a stew pot over an open fire. When she stumbled and dropped her utensils, Robin bent over to pick them up with a smile.

Anslee waited for them to move on before saying, "The woods were never safe, Robin. You and I both know that. There was that time we were almost bit by a wolf, the other time we almost got our legs caught in a hunter's trap, and don't even get me started on our time running from bees." She laughed as she ticked their childhood antics off her fingers one by one, recounting all the times they had survived in their not-quite-safe forest.

"No, no, not like that. Of course, the dangers of nature have always been present." He paused a moment to hold back a tree branch for her to walk through. She blushed, remembering how she had hated when he had done that to her when they were kids. She had always wanted him to see her as his equal, despite being years younger. "What is happening now is more than that. It's as if... predators are waiting for us each night. Holding themselves back on the edges of the woods and waiting for the right moment to pounce. At first, we thought it was wolves, but we haven't been able to find any concrete evidence."

Her mind jumped to the shadow creature she had seen in the town. Could Robin be seeing something similar?

"That sounds terrifying," Anslee whispered before chastising herself. Robin and her had their own run-in with a wolf. They had stumbled upon a lone wolf out hunting, close enough to camp that adults had come running when they tried to scare it away by shouting. But they had encountered nothing magical out here before. To imagine anything dark and shadowy creeping through these woods seemed silly with the sunlight streaming overhead.

"Yes, it does," he agreed solemnly. "It started a few months ago. The feeling has been growing stronger these past few weeks. It has become almost unbearable with the worry and anxiety it causes for all the people. They can barely stand to enter the towns anymore."

"Just from worry? That sounds a little unbelievable." She fingered her necklace, remembering her own fear over the shadow wolf... and her reluctance to share that fear with anyone else. Especially since she had decided it hadn't even been real. And here she was no better than what she had feared, denying fear the roamers may have truly had.

"It is not just worry," he sighed. "The emotions run deeper than that. This feeling... is magical."

She scoffed at him. "Impossible! Magic doesn't exist." Although after Cria's warnings, Magda's old tales, and that brief flash with Avery in the dress shop, perhaps it did.

"That's the thing, though. There used to be magic in this kingdom, Lee! I remember it. You may have been too young, but there used to be magic here. Magic steeped the land. Almost every person could feel it."

She couldn't stand another person insisting magic was real. It couldn't be. It simply didn't fit into her life in Yonderton.

"Do you think your tall tales will keep me here listening to you longer?" Anslee crossed her arms and stopped walking, angry now. She had already wasted a complete night out here. She didn't want to lose her morning too. "I would know if magic had been here. We would all know. People would miss it, or talk about it, or tell stories about it at the very least..." But Magda had told her stories...

"Have you ever wondered why they haven't?" Robin insisted. "Just because you do not listen nor believe, does not mean they are not told. Think about it, Lee. And if you want to see for yourself, come back tonight, and I will show you this is not mass paranoia."

Robin was certainly persistent. And dedicated to his theory. She wondered if he had always been this stubborn as a child, and she was too enamored to notice. But his stubbornness now was not endearing. It was angering her, forcing her to face what she had been too eager to hide away. She didn't want to come back to the woods. She didn't want to face the truth anymore than she wanted to hear that magic had indeed returned to the mountains and lands of Yonderton.

He stopped just outside the town borders, where the dense foliage gradually gave way to a beaten path, and bowed slightly. She thought the gesture ironic but held her tongue.

"Think about what I said, Lee, and come tonight. We will be waiting."

She knew she wouldn't be back. But she didn't tell him that. She walked away without looking back.

22

Anslee slipped inside the house, hoping to head up to her room with no one seeing her in this state. Unfortunately, Magda was waiting for her right inside the kitchen. Not sure why she expected anything different. Magda was always in the kitchen, doing the chores that were required of her. She sighed half-heartedly.

"Stay somewhere last night?" Magda asked her, not moving from her station at the kitchen counter. Anslee brought her hand up to her hair, gently feeling around yesterday's mussed doo. She pulled out some twigs and leaves and stared at them before dropping them on the floor.

"Pick those up before leaving the kitchen."

Cursing to herself, she bent down to the ground and picked up the twigs.

"Go clean up and change your clothes. Then come back down here and finish helping me." Her words were terse, her tone cold. She had never seen the old woman so angry.

Anslee trudged upstairs, careful not to shed any other debris on her way. She shed her clothes and left them in a heap on her floor. At least she did not need to keep this room clean. She switched her dirty blue dress for a pale ivory undershirt. She wanted to hide in normal sleep clothes in her own bed, not face the new day with secret revelations of magic. Remind herself that she was her own person now, not beholden to the customs and superstitions of the roamers. She wanted to wash away the stink from last night's ill-fated adventure.

She redid her hair, brushing it through with her fingers before hastily braiding it up again and tucking the ends into the side of her braid closest to her scalp. Regretfully, she hung her red cloak up against the back of the door. She brushed off all the loose dirt and tiny sticks caught in the thread. Dirt stains spotted the scarlet fabric. The coat would need a good soak. And then there was the deep rip in the left sleeve that was stained with blood. She sighed. That would certainly need more attention to fix. Robin had ensured Crio cleaned and re-wrapped her stitches before they left the roamers' camp, but had done nothing for her cloak. Tidy clothes weren't a priority for roamers. But they were for her. A problem to deal with after a nap and appeasing Magda.

Unfortunately, she had not made it to her bed before Georgie found her.

"My... my lady," he stammered, bowing. It was a habit he had taken upon himself once Avery had called on her regularly in the afternoons. He thought it gave her a certain honor just by being associated with him, and ignored Anslee when she insisted she was still just a maid. She motioned for him to rise, exasperated with his antics and not in the mood to be patient with him.

"What? Is Avery here?" she asked.

He nodded.

"Well, tell him I cannot see him. There is simply too much to be done today." She couldn't very well explain why she was still in her nightclothes or that she had just returned home. Georgie tried to tell her something about Avery, but Anslee was too tired to pretend to be in a good mood for Avery so early in the day, especially when his existence threatened the fragile hold she had on her sanity and insistence that magic wasn't real. "Send my apologies. Go, now."

He gave a brief bow again, and he was off down the hallway. She slunk into bed, ready for a nap and some beloved respite from unwanted company.

Her door banged open. Anslee jumped out of bed, covering herself with a sheet. A dark form stood backlit by the hallway lights, his hand holding open the door. A moment and her eyes adjusted. Avery! She cringed. What was he doing here? She didn't want him to see where she lived.

"You refused to see me," he said.

She could have sworn his eyes flashed in the dark.

"I wasn't prepared," she stuttered, gesturing to her dressing gown. She didn't need to mention the guilt she felt about running off into the woods, even if it hadn't been by her own choosing.

He paused, slowly eyeing the thin dressing gown she wore. She had never thought it so revealing, but heat flushed across her skin. He seemed to regain a sense of propriety and looked away.

"My apologies, my dear." His calm voice was back, and he inhaled as if fighting for control over his emotions. "I forget myself sometimes. I am so used to being obeyed..." He trailed off. "But you would let me know if you were toying with me, wouldn't you?" he asked, suddenly intent. "I couldn't bear it if you were the object of another's affections." He reminded her of a cat waiting to pounce again, waiting for her to make one wrong move. She wondered if he could somehow sense where she had been. Did she smell like the open air and mossy grounds of the woods?

Could this be the misstep he was waiting for? The chance for him to end their dalliance without shame?

She pulled the covers around her closer, protecting herself and her secrets.

"I'm resting," she snapped, going on the offensive. "You obviously know I'm not wealthy, Lord Varrock." She threw his title back in his face. He blinked. "I live here, in this tiny room, and support the true owners here. I'm a tool to be used. Are you happy now? Is this what you wanted? To see the squalor I live in?"

He recoiled, noticing for the first time the dinginess of the room. The healthy plants that thrived near the small window, the only decoration, the barren vanity and small bed she huddled against.

"Not fit for a queen..." he mumbled.

"If you hadn't noticed, I'm not your queen," she said darkly.

He snapped his fingers and transported them to a plush bedroom. Silken green drapes covered highly arched walls and light streamed in through floor to ceiling windows. Greenery covered every open surface and elaborate gowns peeped through an open closet larger than her room. A golden crown gleamed atop a pedestal in a corner. In a moment, the vision was gone.

"What was that?" Anslee whispered, her heart in her throat.

Avery recomposed himself. It was as if the angry, haughty lord no longer existed. He wrapped his magic around himself, drawing all the power he had drenched the room in back into himself.

Oh no.

"What if you could be?" he muttered so quietly she didn't know if she had imagined it. He took a step closer, but she threw out her arms, blocking him.

"No closer!" she cried. The thought of the magic overwhelmed her. She gripped the blanket closer, as if the measly thread count could protect her. In the window's light, she saw cruel, jagged marks over Avery's skin, as if a wild beast had raked him. They were raw and pink - new.

"A shadow wolf," she whispered incoherently.

His sharp eagle eyes took in the locket atop the vanity, the bright red cloak stained with blood. Avery inhaled deeply, and his eyes flashed. He stalked over to the cape and picked it up.

"Who hurt you?" he demanded. His eyes promised retribution.

"I'm not hurt," she denied automatically, curling in on herself. She didn't want to show any weakness in front of him, and she prayed he couldn't tell she favored her right arm. Her gut was telling her he wasn't safe.

He considered her a moment. "I see that I've scared you. That was not my intention. I'll leave you now. Please, feel better, my dear." He bowed low before sweeping out of the room. Her skin shivered when he called her dear. She didn't feel precious to him. She felt like his property.

Anslee had debated whether or not it was wise to meet Robin. She had wanted to stick her head in the sand and pretend that magic didn't exist. That no one was looking for her. Instead, the magic had found her.

She couldn't pretend any longer.

23

The woods were dark, brooding and unsure of her being there. It almost felt as if the trees themselves were alive, judging her and her worthiness to stay. Anslee scoffed at the thought. She had been born and raised in woods like these. If anyone had the authority to walk amongst these wooded paths, it was her.

The night sky grew darker, and the happy chattering of the nocturnal woodland creatures faded away as Anslee walked farther in the woods. She felt less confident now and second guessed her decision to walk alone and without telling even Magda where she was going. She had not known Robin since she was a child. Could she really trust him now?

But even if she could not trust him, seeing him had brought back other memories of running through the woods and stumbling on buried treasure. Now she wondered if that part had been real or a figment of an overactive childhood imagination. Even if there was just a chance that her memory of a hidden crown had been real... she had to see. Such riches would lead to money, and money would help her establish a dowry, thus securing her future in society. She would never be forced to wander again. Of course, Robin did not need to know all this. It is sufficient for him to think she has come to him solely to see the haunted woods he has promised her.

She had almost reached the spot where Robin accosted her yesterday when she heard a slight rustling and jumped. She had been expecting Robin to retrieve her, but she still tensed when she saw him step outside of the forest behind her. He raised his hands, a bow in his right hand and an arrow and quiver on his back.

"Not armed tonight."

She raised her eyebrows.

"Well, not aimed at you tonight," he corrected.

"Small gifts," she conceded. "So let's get on with it. Aren't you supposed to be showing me something dreadful tonight?" She kept her tone light, hiding her anxiety to get the night over, and see if he had been telling the truth or not.

"Yes, I am. Although you will see for yourself soon enough." He glanced around the forest at them, nervously confirming no one else was within range. She wondered what he had to feel nervous about.

"You certainly took your time getting here tonight," Robin told her. He peered at her when she walked a little closer, and he could see her more clearly. "I see you left your necklace at home this time." His hands brushed against her bare throat, and she jerked away at his unexpected touch, slapping his hand away.

"Don't touch me," she snapped. She would never admit it, but she felt safer walking beside him. Thoughts of magic and her confrontation with Avery swam through her mind. She didn't want anyone touching her.

She had removed Avery's gift before heading out for the night, anxious about the warning she had received from Crio the night before. She had uncovered Robin's necklace from her dresser and held it in her palms for a short while, debating whether or not she should wear it. Eventually, she had determined switching necklaces felt too much like declaring allegiance, and she had foregone any jewelry altogether. She had not expected Robin, or anyone, to notice so soon.

"It did not seem prudent to wear it tonight," she said, gripping her hands together to keep from touching the naked hollow of her throat. Thinking of the necklaces had her remembering how she had first run into Robin a few weeks ago. "Robin, can you be honest with me?"

"Yes, of course." He hurried them through the woods but slowed down to walk beside her. His hazel eyes glowed as they focused on her. Could she really accuse him of this? Her oldest friend?

"Did you steal that locket you gave me that day?" She almost whispered the question, not wanting to believe it of him. His pace slowed considerably at her words, although he did not quit pushing them forward.

"I never planned on turning into one of them. You know that, Anslee. You had to have known." He pushed a few branches aside, pushing her forward with his hand on her elbow, keeping her from tripping over fallen branches. They had always been alike in their disdain for those roamers who turned to thievery. "But with everything that's been going on, and the fear instilled in everyone lately, there was no other option. Almost everyone refuses to leave the camp out of fear, and what sort of leader would I be if I pushed everyone outside their boundaries? No, they would simply freeze in fear, if not worse."

"What are you leading, exactly?" she asked him and could not stop whispering.

He looked surprised at her question. "The people. The roamers. They are... too scared to lead themselves. And when they found us, and how we were trying to deal with the epidemic, they just came. I'd say we've doubled in size since the time I first saw you. It's become harder to ensure everyone has what they need, and we've been rationing our goods. However, we do our best, and I'll take care of those who can't take care of themselves. They are good people, Lee. It's not their fault what's been happening to the land and to them." She noticed he never answered her question.

He shifted away from her. "I guess I ended up just like the rest of the roamers after all." He swung the last branch of the forest wide, revealing the fire beyond, just as the sun finished setting behind him. She could not see his face, but she imagined with his awkward stance that he was uncomfortable with his last statement.

"No, Robin. No, not at all. You are nothing like the rest of them," she murmured to him. He had taken care of her yesterday, then insisted that she join him today to learn the truth. From what she remembered, roamers were isolationists. No one else would have taken the time to help her. And by his own admission, he stole to keep his people fed. She had to make him understand she believed he stayed true to his ideals. It was important to her. Maybe if he could see that he was more than the worse of him, then she could be too.

"No one else would do what you have done. Go against everything you stand for. Taking care of others that are too scared to take care of themselves. It's heroic what you've been doing for everyone." They walked right up to the edge of the fire, and the warmth from the flames licked her side as she faced Robin. She felt comfortable standing here in the warmth with him. He gazed intently at her, soaking up every word she said. His hands stroked her upper arms, careful to avoid her injury, and her breath caught in her throat.

"Did you think I needed to hear that?" he asked with a small smile.

A soft breeze drifted their way from the forest, and it caused the air on the top of her arms to prickle. Had that originated in the forest? It had been a calm, windless day today, and she had expected more of the same tonight. She wrapped her arms around herself, trying to regain a little body heat.

Robin's eyes narrowed. "Have you felt it then? The magic is rising." Her skin prickled ominously at his words. He had claimed magic was here, but she had been loath to believe him. After this morning... she was less certain he was mistaken.

Robin led her over to a few seats that lined the fireplace. "We'll wait here for the night. The fire will offer us some protection, as will the circle. I'm sorry to force this upon you, but it is the only way you will learn for yourself." He gestured toward the thin silver circle that surrounded them, salt sprinkled religiously around them. Another old wives' tale, she thought, that may have a grain of truth in it.

She bristled at his words, though. She wasn't a child receiving a lesson. "I asked for this, Robin. Don't patronize me. I need to know what you have been experiencing out here, if only..." She trailed off, unsure how much she could admit to him.

"If only what, Lee?"

She bit her lip, not wanting to let out the truth that festered inside her. "If only to trust you again," she whispered.

He nodded slowly. "I thought as much. These are hard times, Lee, and I have had to make hard decisions. But I want you to understand. I want you to know what is coming after us so you will know how to prepare yourself or how to let me protect you." He reached up and tucked a loose piece of hair back into the braid wrapped around her head. His fingers lingered against her cheek until she reached up and wrapped her own hand in his. She gently pulled his hand down away from her face, and it landed in her lap, nestled in her palms. His touch was tender and kind, but she needed to be strong on her own in case he spoke the truth about the magic. She had to stand on her own two feet.

She smiled at him. "You have good instincts, Robin. You know I would never let you try to protect me if I did not perceive the threat myself." He scooted a little closer to her and tugged her against him until they sat shoulder to shoulder. She had worn her old cloak, and it crinkled and crunched between them, keeping her as warm as he did.

They fell into their old patterns easily, innately comfortable around one another, if still prickly. Their backs faced the fire and warmed them from the outside. They stared across the dark expanse of the tree line, waiting to see what the night would bring.

24

Anslee knew when the creatures arrived. Adrenaline pulsed through her veins, although there was no enemy to fight. This was more than just the nervous apprehension she felt when walking the dark corridors of the city capital. This was the slow wait for an enemy that wanted to pounce on her. Her blood sizzled, sparking and bubbling against her, wanting to rebel against her silent wait. She gripped Robin's hand so hard her knuckles turned white. She leaned in closer. "How do you not scream?"

"Do not whisper, Lee. It gives them more power over your fear." Robin spoke in a calm, rational tone, although more subdued than his normal voice.

"I whisper for fear that if I do not, then I shall scream," she hissed back at him, jumping up to release the nervous energy flooding her body. Her right shoulder twitched. Tiny pinpricks razed her body, and the hair on the back of her neck stood up. She felt the anxiety of a hundred country judges staring down at her, making her feel small and condemning her to her worst fears. "I do not feel fear. I feel alarm! Trumpets of warning are blaring inside my skull. I don't want to sit back and let this... this unknown take over me! I need to fight! But where is my enemy? Who is it that threatens me? I do not know, and this not knowing drives me mad, Robin. Absolutely mad. How can you stand this?" She whirled to him unexpectedly, pointing her finger at his chest. "How can you just sit by and not go in there? Let your people succumb to this unknown and abject terror?" Shadows from the fire danced against them, throwing silhouettes of flames against the woods beyond them.

"Who are you?" she demanded, whirling to face the darkness, and walking up to the edges of their protective salt circle. "Why do you come here and threaten our lands? Disturb our people? What gives you that right?" Now she was shouting, gesturing and stomping at the trees as Robin pulled her back from stepping over the salt circle, trying to keep her closer to the protective light of the fire.

She had expected no answers, so she jumped back when a multitude of whispering, hissing voices filled the night air.

"We are the abandoned..."

"The tortured..."

"The bereft..."

"The slain..."

"The returned..."

"We have come back..."

"To conquer..."

"To expel..."

"To eradicate..."

"To rewrite what should never have happened."

"Who are you...?"

"Little princess..."

"Little prince..."

"Little unknown?"

"Nothing."

"Nothing."

"No one..."

"...and nothing."

Vivid amber, ochre, and citrine eyes glared at them from the darkness. Robin tensed against her, waiting to see if this would be the night the stalemate ended, and these unknown creatures swarmed and attacked them.

Anslee stumbled backward, tripping over Robin's frantic pulling, and they crashed into the fire, flames blazing around them. He rolled her over, out of the flames, back and forth, right and left. Her throat locked, and she breathed in and out through her nose. In. Out. In. Out. In. In. In. Her eyes squeezed shut. She was losing control of her own breath.

Dense, olive-green fog rolled across them, sliding past their barrier, making it harder to see. As it faded, it took the whispers with them. Anslee felt immense terror, trapped within the dense fog, unable to see or hear around her. Shadows rolled off her, squirming along the ground around them.

Robin slapped her, jarring her into consciousness. She inhaled great gulps of clean air. They had rolled past the fire and the salt line, but it seemed the ominous magic was gone. She swallowed more air. Fresh air. Crisp with the scent of pine. The whispering had stopped. The unnatural shadows were gone.

Robin grabbed Anslee's arm hard and yanked her to him, turning on his heel to walk toward the center of their camp.

Guards he had placed on the perimeter came to attention as Robin strode through the camp and began barking orders. "Put more wood on these fires! Get every person into their tents tonight! I want no one else out except those on perimeter duty! Call back anyone that has left to scout the area." Immediately, people jumped into action, doing his bidding. No one questioned his motives or reasons, but he told them anyway. "The creatures have gone on the verbal offensive tonight. We believe they may try an aggressive, physical attack as well, although I am not convinced that they will. Either way, we shall be prepared. Notify me at once if anyone hears them again." He took Anslee and stormed into what must be his tent in the center of the frenzy.

He whirled her around to look at him. She had remained quiet during the entire ordeal, but she wondered if he could read the thoughts flashing wildly in her mind. "Did anyone else hear that?" he asked her hoarsely, not able to let all the emotions he felt run away with him just yet.

"How would I know?" she snarled.

"And you are unharmed?" he asked.

She looked down at her soot-stained clothing. "You saw for yourself! No one attacked me, at least not physically..."

"And mentally?" He restrained himself from rushing over to her and running his hands over her, checking for himself to make sure she had sustained no injuries.

"No," she snapped. "At least, I think not." She paused for a moment to mentally check herself. "But I'm barely holding it together." This was said much softer than the first, as the adrenaline of the night leaked away and the cold, hard reality set in. She wrapped her arms around herself, grateful for the old cloak that withstood the flames.

"Good," he whispered back. Then he rushed her, hands running up and down her arms, reassuring himself that she was fine, and her body was warm underneath his fingertips. She reciprocated his investigation, and soon his hands were softly cradling her head, tilting her back so he could lightly kiss her on the lips. Her lips were soft against his, and her whole body paused. But then she was kissing him back, gently at first, then fiercely, with a fervor he quickly matched.

She was alive and safe, and the adrenaline had coursed through her body when Robin rushed her. She came alive under his touch, achingly aware that she needed to be held and needed to be lost in the arms of someone to keep her mind off the creatures in the woods. This was nothing like kissing Avery. This was safety and a fierce determined need to prove they were both alive, they were both safe. They were both electrifyingly aware of the other. Robin pulled her closer to him, and she wrapped her hands around his neck, pressing his thighs against hers, his chest against her chest. She was lost in the moment and did not know how long she stood there with him, their bodies pressed against each other, fervently exploring the taste and feel of each other.

"Oh, Lee," he took a moment to whisper against her lips when she came up for breath. "I am so glad no one else was there to hear. Your secret is always safe with me." She froze inside his arms, then took a step back. What was he talking about? Did he know about Avery's magic?

"What secret?" She arched an eyebrow, her voice icy.

"Your... the... the past. Your past," he finished lamely.

"You know my past. Almost every person here does. I grew up here, with the village brats. I am one of you," she said softly, hating to admit it out loud.

"You and I both know that is not true," Robin whispered.

"I am not so sure that I do." No matter how far she ran, she would always be a roamer at heart. Look how quickly she had let herself become entangled in the roamers' affairs.

"Why are you being so complicated? Lee, just let me in!" Robin growled and ran his hands through his hair, further mussing the brown strands. "Wouldn't it be easier if you opened up to me? I can help you figure out what is going on!"

"Nothing is going on here!" Anslee shouted back, breaking the nonverbal agreement for a whispered, almost silent match they had been competing in. At her shout, several guards rushed through the tent flap and into their argument. It certainly looked like there had been something going on here. Robin straightened his shoulders, adjusting his tunic and quiver still strung along his back. At a few curious glances, Anslee realized her own disheveled appearance. Robin had pulled her entire braid undone and her dress was rumpled, her eyes wild. She ignored the guards, turning away to sort herself out and pretend the roamers' affairs were none of her business.

"Sir?" His chief guard stepped forward, glancing between the two of them. "Is everything okay here?"

He nodded sharply. "Yes, of course. Thank you for checking. Any noticeable differences on the perimeter?"

The guard second shook his head. Negative. He threw a questioning look at Anslee's backside but did not ask questions. Instead, he returned to the two who had barged in. "Return to your posts, men. Nothing to see here." The three of them trouped out. The tent flat closed fully before Robin turned to address Anslee again, but she held up her hand in front of her face. No doubt he wanted to harass her again.

"No, no, no. Just stop, Robin."

She was angry. Her stance was square against him, and her face flushed, not with the emotions behind their embrace, but with a fierce determination to tell him off.

"I think I've heard enough of what you have to say. I came out here to listen to your explanation and see for myself, and I have. I believe you. There are... things out there. But I have seen enough, and I am ready to leave."

He should know arguing with her would be hopeless.

"I can't risk anyone helping you return home tonight. Not now that we've heard those creatures. You'll have to stay here again. Come with me, and you can sleep where you stayed last time."

Anslee kept her distance as she followed Robin to the bedroll she had previously used, angry at how he had taken advantage of her heightened emotional state. She would leave at dawn. It was time to go back to keeping her distance from Robin.

25

Avery had a surprise for Anslee when he called on her that afternoon. She opened the door herself, since Georgie had been trying not to cry upon learning the day's bad news. She herself was trying not to dwell on Magda's revelation.

If it surprised Avery to see her answering the door, he did not show it. Just turned his lips up in a cheeky grin and gestured to the two saddled horses behind him. "Surprise, my dear! I thought we might take a stroll in the nearby woods today... on horseback!"

Anxiety rushed through her at his news (The woods! Robin! The last two nights she had spent there!), but she kept her true feelings from showing on her face. But she had been ignoring her feelings for Robin and her fear of the shadows. Perhaps confronting the area in the light of day would replace her fear with fresh memories.

"How delightful. I'll need to change into riding attire. Won't you rest in the parlor while I change?" She hurried him inside the manor. She could tell Avery was pleased with himself for he spoke about the joys of horseback riding while he followed her. He obviously didn't know she had been raised astride horses, constantly moving from place to place with the roamers. Normally he was much more in tune with her feelings, and she was secretly relieved Avery didn't pick up on her apprehension. She offered a slice of pie she had baked earlier to keep herself distracted from her guilt, but he refused. He brushed aside her attempts to offer him some tea or coffee while he waited, eager for her to get on with changing so they could leave.

She took her time picking out her outfit for the day's riding. She told herself it was because she wanted to look her best for a day Avery was obviously so excited for, even though deep down she knew she was avoiding him a little longer. Feelings of guilt nibbled on the edges of her conscience, but she did her best to keep them away. She spritzed perfume - a rare luxury - on her wrists and along her neck. She would smell like horse and woods all day. Best to smell a little fresher if Avery got close. She finally settled on some tan riding breeches, dark brown boots and a navy riding jacket. These were probably out of fashion, but she didn't have many clothing choices to choose from, and these had come from rummaging around in the attic years earlier. Back when the old woman had still been alive and delighted Anslee with tales of sneaking off to ride bareback through the woods, she had pulled out trunks of old mementos to show her. Much later, after the old woman had passed away, Anslee had snuck back up into the attic, pulling out the clothes and trinkets the lady had shared with her, and secretly kept a few for herself, like the riding clothes.

She lightly stepped down the stairs, trying to keep her boots from clunking. Avery stood abruptly as she walked in. He frowned immediately upon seeing her.

"Where is your necklace?"

She had forgotten she had removed it for her secret rendezvous in the woods. She hesitated before answering. "I thought I would leave it off for the ride. I am sure the terrain will be rougher than just walking, and I did not want it to clunk against my chest while we rode."

"You should go put it back on." Although his words sounded like a suggestion, she could tell from his tone it was not. It was a demand. She debated fighting with him over it, but guilt over her last two nights away flashed through her.

At her hesitation, his voice grew gentler. "It has protective properties. Please wear it. For me."

She caved and went back upstairs to retrieve her bloodstone necklace. She cringed as it settled against the concave of her neck. It looked incredibly dashing against her creamy white blouse and navy blazer, but she could already imagine how uncomfortable it would be while they rode. Her reflection stared back at her, passing judgment before she returned downstairs. She saw a pale, withdrawn, unhappy woman. She groaned. Oh, what she would do to alleviate the guilt of omission.

She came back down the stairs again, not bothering to hide the noise from her steps. He grinned at her.

"Let us go then!" He strode toward the door, grabbing her as he went. She spun after him, giggling. In the light of the day, he looked suave and charming. She couldn't reconcile the excited man in front of her with the demanding one that had towered over her the other night. She refused to believe that had really been him.

In no time he had them on their horses and bounding out towards the woods. To her surprise, he had pulled out a large silk scarf before mounting and tucked it around her neck. "It is nippy out today, so this will protect against the bite of cold. It should also keep your necklace from bouncing around too much." He winked at her, his face inches from her own as he placed the scarf around her shoulders. She thought he would lean down to sneak a quick kiss, and she waited expectantly, but he just pulled away and offered his hands to give her a boost into the saddle.

They galloped through the woods, the wind streaming past their ears. She pulled to a stop as she felt her scarf loosen and break free. It fluttered in the wind for a moment before flying completely free from her neck, rising in the wind and buffeted about. She chased after it, but Avery pulled up beside her to stop her.

"Let it go, dear," he told her. "I meant it for your comfort."

She bit her lip. "Oh, Avery. I can not just take your things from you! Please let me go retrieve it. I cannot pay you back."

He gestured at the empty sky around them. "And where will you go, my love? Do you see it anywhere in this clearing?" She twisted her neck to look about them. But indeed, the scarf had vanished, blown away by the wind and probably hidden somewhere along the dozens of leaves they had just trampled through. She grunted in frustration, and the horse she was atop stomped its foot, sensing her frustration. "If only I could go after it," she mumbled.

"Why are you so bothered by this?" Avery looked cross, as if she was ruining his pleasantly planned afternoon.

"It is just... oh! You may as well know. The manor is being closed up and our lord is leaving back to the countryside. I will be out of a job soon, not even able to pretend to be the sort of high lady you deserve." She looked off to the side, refusing to look at him and trying to let the tears keep from leaking out of her eyes. Their lord no longer felt safe in the city after the recent attacks, and unlike her, he had the resources and fortunes to escape to the far-off countryside. And instead of looking for a new job, here she was off flirting with Avery again, getting nowhere. Maybe she would end up a roamer again after all.

Perhaps it was being deep in the woods without mention of civilization. Perhaps it was the consistent rendezvous with Robin. But she thought of the other time she had found hidden treasures in these woods. She wondered if the crown she had stumbled upon with Robin so long ago was still hidden here. With the reward announced, that would certainly give her enough riches to survive the rest of her life in peace. She shivered at the thought. She didn't want to invite any more magic into her life, not when it was not supposed to exist.

She turned to face away from Avery again, since she had not been listening to what he was saying, and he was trying to put his face in front of hers. Off to the left, yes, it felt like something was calling to her from there. That could be a place to start... it almost felt as if she was being tugged along. She turned her horse to head that way, when Avery's next words had her jerking back to him, almost out of her seat.

"Marry me."

Her jaw dropped as she stared at him, speechless. He had gotten off his horse, and it waited patiently behind him, watching them with big, brown eyes. He stood before her, hands at his sides, and sauntered up to her, taking her horse's bridle to keep her from running away again. Thoughts of finding a long-lost treasure vanished from her mind.

"But what will people think?" She was embarrassed that these were the first words that sprang to her mind.

"Does it matter? I'll give you your own place. We do not have to stop seeing each other. You will not need to worry about anything ever again, Anslee. Do you realize that? Do you realize what I am offering?"

Safety. Protection. A permanent home. How could she say yes to any of those things when she had nothing to offer in return? She opened her mouth to resist again, but nothing came out. He came around the side of her horse, gripping her leg. "Say nothing just yet. If you cannot answer yes, then I ask you to think this over before giving me your answer. I could give you everything you have ever dreamed of, Anslee. Riches beyond your wildest dreams. A life of comfort. Love and companionship for all your days. Please." His hand reached up to curl around her own, which had curled tightly against her thigh. "At least consider me."

What's holding me back? I thought this was what I wanted. A permanent home. A place to call my own and set down roots.

She nodded slowly. “I think I should return home,” she murmured. “My head. It hurts. This has all just been so much to take in.” He sighed, but murmured his agreement. He jumped back on his horse to lead her home.

This situation with Magda and their lord had taught her she couldn’t come to a home empty-handed, or that’s how she would leave. She had arrived a poor beggar child, and without Avery to fall back on, she would leave a poor, beggar woman. She needed funds to protect herself and claim the stability being offered. She would turn in the crown for the reward and have enough of her own funds to make her the sort of woman that Avery deserved. Tonight.

She would come back to look for the crown tonight.

26

Avery

"The usurpers? I've taken care of them," his Queen told him. A cruel smile spread across her face as she lounged on a velvet chaise.

A shiver traveled down Avery's spine. His queen's emotions overshadowed both the cool evening air and raging fire within the palace.

"My Queen," Avery said, taking her hand and bowing low over it. "Sometimes you frighten me with your passion."

She smirked. "As I ought to," she said haughtily.

"Our first phase of the plan has been a success. You've claimed your place as the rightful heir. A larger retinue of our people are taking their places, seeping into everyday society. The attacks are working. Our shadows have reported that the townsfolk are fearful. They will look for a strong ruler to guide them."

"And the girl?" she asked sharply. "What of her?"

Avery hesitated. He had hoped Anslee would have led him to the crown. After all, she should have had an innate connection with it given the circumstances of her birth. Yet, so far, she had proved useless. She knew less than nothing about the innate magic of the land. She barely understood her own nation's politics. What had started as a side quest to further please and empower his queen had grown stale. But he was not ready to give it up yet... There were glimmers she could still prove useful.

"Avery! I'm not keen on waiting." His queen's voice had grown cold and withdrawn. She had little patience, his queen. And she was quick to strike once angered. He drew his magic to him like a shield. Not too much, less her attack proves weak and he anger her further. But he wanted to protect his vital organs, at least.

Her magic reached out and smacked him, a smart rebuke. He winced, but held his ground.

"Take care of the girl," she commanded. "Having her alive threatens our plans. The land can never fully be mine if she lives. And if we cannot find the crown..." Her voice drifted off. "Make sure she's taken care of, Avery. Like her parents." He couldn't mention that he had claimed her. Not now, when it would anger his queen further.

He had placed his queen on the throne. But she had grown more powerful since she arrived. Soon he could no longer defeat her in a show of strength. He had been pulling the strings since before they journeyed here, but now, with the land's true power within reach, the puppet was surpassing the puppet master.

Avery bowed. "Yes, my Queen. Of course." He would have to hide Anslee from her. It was the only way to keep her—and him—safe.

27

After days of unsuccessful searches, Anslee gave up on finding the crown again. It had been foolish to think she could walk into the woods and stumble upon it as easily as when she was a child. If it had been so easy to find years ago, then someone else must have realized its worth and pawned it by now.

Now she stood beside Avery at another ball in the palace, delicately nibbling on macaroons, trying her best to avoid the well-dressed ladies of court shooting daggers at her as they walked past and gossiped behind their fans. Avery had finally invited her to one of the social gatherings he was privy to as high advisor to Their Majesties. This was the first ball he had invited her to since the Midsummer Ball, which was now called the Triumphant Return of Our Lady.

He had insisted it would be a "small affair," but that did not fool her. There were as many people here as crowded Market Row every Sunday. She wore the first gown Avery had ever gifted her, cleaned as best as she could after its multiple stains. She was glad she had saved it, and not salvaged it for parts after all. It was still the fanciest dress she owned.

She had not forgotten her night standing with Robin against the shadow beasts. She had been sneaking out after her morning chores and time with Avery, to give her plenty of time to search and be back before true dark fell. She did not want whatever had spoken to her in the woods to come back and find her. Magda had been gossiping about more criminals being jailed than usual, so she was also eager to have Anslee safe at home before dark. Anslee had faked headaches each day, so now Avery thought she was avoiding him as well, after his awkward declaration of intending to marry her. His proposal sat heavy between them.

At least, until today. At least she wore her necklace against the courtly finery. Since Avery's anger with her, she was extra careful to ensure it was always on her neck when he was around.

Her trepidation must have irritated Avery, for he had finally lashed out at her. "Dear god, Anslee. How long will you keep me waiting? Either commit to me or not! Have I not given you everything you desired?"

She had paused, a sweet treat raised halfway to her mouth. It must have been a comical scene for the other attendees, but everyone nearby had conveniently looked the other way when Avery raised his voice.

He was angrier than she would have expected. What spurred him on? As if he sensed her hesitation at his anger, his voice became gentle. He took Anslee's hand and stroked it gently between his. She gasped at the soft caress of her sensitive palms. His fingernails tickled the lifeline that spanned her left palm and inner wrist. *A fact you know from the roamers*, an annoying part of her mind voiced.

"I worry for your safety, my dear," he whispered into her ear, stepping closer. Heat emanated from him, making her shiver. "With my position so near my Queen, I cannot take risks without worrying about you. Every day you are not at my side, my worry increases."

Her breath hitched. She had never imagined there may be a more sinister reason for Avery's proposal. That he worried those besides himself had ulterior, nefarious motives.

This game of cat-and-mouse was drawing to a close. Whatever else she was waiting for was not coming. Her searches for the crown had proved fruitless. Perhaps she should have taken Robin up on his offer all those weeks ago to search for the crown together. But it was too late now. Avery offered her a home and stability, which she would desperately need in a few days' time.

"You are right, Robin, of course. It has been silly of me to wait this long to answer you." He had asked her to marry him knowing she did not have a dowry. He would never know she had wished for something different.

His face darkened. "Who. Is. Robin." He growled between clenched teeth.

Oh.

"Just a childhood friend. I am so sorry, Avery. Of course, I meant you!"

He glared at her, icy daggers piercing his gaze. She reached out a hand to grasp his, silently beseeching him to trust her, much as he had that day in the woods over a week ago. Woods where a week and a day ago, Robin had caressed her under the stars.

His eyes flashed, and he visibly restrained himself as she caressed his hand. "Yes, of course. How silly of me to get jealous of a simple slip of the tongue," he murmured. He pulled his hand away and reached into his pocket to produce a small box. "I have been carrying this with me ever since our first conversation. Waiting for you, Anslee. I will always wait for you." He popped it open, and nestled inside the black velvet was an elaborate ring. A gold band with another cluster of bloodstones at its apex.

An engagement ring.

He slid the ring over her finger and Anslee trembled. What were these stones signifying death and hardship and pain dripping over her body? Avery insisted he enjoyed them for their rarity, but she could not get Crio and Robin's warnings out of her mind.

To her further surprise, Avery claimed to have a small, intimate engagement party planned for them tomorrow tonight.

"Already?" she questioned suspiciously.

"No, of course not," he laughed. "But everyone has been on standby and I will plan it tonight." He pulled her to him and gave her a light peck on the tip of her nose. All traces of his earlier anger were gone. "I'm glad you wore the violet gown tonight. The first gift I ever gave you."

Her breath caught in her throat. She stepped closer, whispering so no one would hear her. "This is awkward, my lord, but if I may ask about funds for a trousseau... I cannot wear this dress again." He looked her up and down, as if appraising that she wore his gown despite the shabbiness.

He nodded. "My good man Chance will see to it. At the very least, you will need a new dress for tomorrow." Avery handed her off to his butler, who silently appeared at Avery's side. "Chance will see to your attire needs while I finish preparations. Goodbye, my dear." He bent low over her hand, and gave her the lightest of kisses against her knuckles before handing her off to Chance.

Back at home, she stood in her room alone, surveying her lackluster dresses. This was what she wanted, wasn't it? To bag a lord. Drape herself in riches and jewels so she never had to worry about going hungry or running for her life ever again. To be sated and well cared for... to be safe. But if that's what she always wanted, then why did it hurt so much? Why did her heart feel wooden and heavy? Avery didn't scare her like he used to, but he didn't give her the same butterflies she felt around a certain not-to-be-named roamer. He didn't push her buttons, anger her, push her to be a better person, or question her decision or worldview. He used her like a walking, talking encyclopedia. She was just another thing to be used by him. But she would be a safe thing.

Would that be enough for her?

28

She arrived downstairs promptly at seven the next evening. Georgie had informed her that he would escort her to the party himself, of all things. She wondered why Avery would not be coming to collect her but assumed it was part of his elaborate plan for the night. He had at least sent his own carriage and guardsmen for her to use, insisting that it was not safe for her to travel alone anymore.

She wore the gown Chance had ordered for her last night. A royal blue twin to the first gown Avery had ever chosen for her. Tiny beads of lapis lazuli encircled the bodice and sleeves, shining brightly in the dim lighting.

The carriage she was in suddenly jerked to a stop, and she realized they were at Avery's town manor. With slight trepidation, she allowed Georgie to escort her out of the carriage and up to a monstrously large house. This was where Avery lived in Yonderton? How had she never been here before? Someone whisked her inside and handed off to the doorman with no time to muse. Trumpets sounded as the doors swung open, and they announced her as "Lady Anslee, the betrothed to Lord Avery, Keeper of the Eastern Whilliswoods." The announcer glared at her over his sheet of paper as she failed to move forward. Apparently she was ruining his job. She hurried forward, scanning to look for Avery in the sea of unrecognizable faces. Small party, he had said. A few people, he had said. People she knew? Now, that he had not specified. She should have asked. Once again, she was thrown into an evening of revelry where she knew no one and kept to the outskirts of the crowd of lords and ladies who gathered together like a congealed unit.

She edged into the crowd, searching for a friendly face, and was surprised to see Magda rush up to her and throw her arms around her. "Oh, my girl! It is so good to see you! I knew you could do it! Bag a lord, I'll be damned! And to think I was worried about finding you a job after this hullabaloo. Why, have you seen the size of this mansion we are in?" She would not stop gabbing, the words pouring from her mouth. Magda was dressed up in her finery from the ball. When had she arrived? And why hadn't they come together? Something had even separated her from her one true friend. This whole event left a sour taste in Anslee's mouth. They were supposed to be celebrating her new life with Avery, and yet she was just... alone.

Anslee smiled meekly and nodded along whenever she felt Magda required an answer. This grand party overwhelmed her. She was thankful to calm her nerves and scope out the party while pretending to listen to Magda. This was a far cry from her humble roamer background. Maybe she didn't know Avery as well as she thought if this is what he considered a small gathering. Her anxiety grew as she walked circles around the room with Magda, grabbing glasses of rosé to calm her nerves. She waited with her safety blanket for a while longer before excusing herself to find Avery. Shouldn't he at least have been there to greet her himself?

She wandered through the room, dodging unknown people and wide columns supporting the cavernous ceiling. She spied Avery in the corner, locked in conversation with another man, their heads bent close together and furiously whispering. Upon coming closer, she realized it was Chance, and that Avery must be giving him some last-minute instructions for the party. She drew closer, meaning to interrupt him for his time and attention. He spun, and locked eyes with her, almost as if he had sensed her approach. Her steps slowed at his gaze, which felt like tiny pinpricks boring into her and she had the sense that her approach had been unwelcome to him.

Where have I felt this before?

Too soon, the moment passed as Avery waved Chance off and turned to greet his fiancée. Now he strode forward boldly, no trace of anger or annoyance on his face, just his calm, self-assured smile. She wondered if that was for the benefit of those around them. Not that their reputation would matter to her, seeing as how she knew no one else here.

"Anslee, my dear," he drew her to him in a light embrace and placed a quick kiss on her cheek. She kept the disappointment from her face - she had expected more.

"You look ravishing tonight. I'm glad Chance gathered this dress last minute. You look resplendent in it." His hands moved to touch the bloodstones at her throat, but then withdrew as if thinking better of it. Perhaps too much impropriety in front of these strangers? She ached with wanting him to touch her, to give her some reassurance of her place beside him.

"You do always seem to know best, my lord." She responded automatically, without the warmth and playfulness of their usual banter. She wanted him to notice and ask what was wrong. To take her aside so it was just the two of them. He didn't do either of these things.

"Hmm, not always," he mused, his lips barely moving apart to let the words out. "Especially when it comes to you." She wondered if he had meant for her to even hear those words. They certainly didn't reassure her about their upcoming nuptials and this awkward party.

"Come, there's someone I want you to meet." He tugged her along, and her interest piqued. She was finally going to meet someone in this crush of strangers. It was worse than the ball she attended for that missing princess. At least there, everyone had been a stranger, and she hadn't felt awkward traipsing around and admiring the grandeur of the palace. Here, she could see all the others mingling with one another, like she was the only outsider. She noticed a few bright eyes on her and Avery as they cut through the crowd, and the tiny hairs along the back of her neck rose in response. She couldn't help a slight shiver, and Avery's hand tightened in response, although he said nothing.

"Here she is, the Lady Moira." Anslee almost ran into Avery's backside as he halted, and peered around him to see the most elegant woman she had ever seen. She wore a fitted mermaid-style blue gown with blond hair loosely pinned back. One gloved hand held a champagne flute, and the other was pressed against Avery's lips. Anslee attempted not to glower. She may have doubts about Avery, but she didn't enjoy sidelining this show. She grumbled as she moved out from behind Avery and was politely ignored by the two others.

"Let me introduce my lovely bride-to-be, the Lady Anslee." Avery stepped aside for the two women to fully scrutinize the other.

"Charmed, I'm sure," the woman called Moira said, dripping condescension. Anslee's fists balled, but she let the comment slide. The woman didn't know Anslee's history or who she was. She couldn't take offense at every little thing. She was here to make nice, after all. At least, she assumed that's what Avery wanted judging by his darkening gaze.

"Delighted," she kept the same snickering undertone the other woman had used. "And how do you two know each other?" If Moira meant to make Anslee feel worthless and less than, then she couldn't let her succeed. Anslee had agreed to Avery's proposal, which meant she belonged here now. It was time to at least pretend to act like it. And if that meant copying this woman's blatant disregard, then that's what she would do.

"We're both advisors to the royal family," Avery said. "It's a sort of family affair, actually. Moira is a distant relation, and we'll be attending the new princess's upcoming coronation. That's why I wanted the two of you to meet. I'll be taking more of a... front role during the proceedings, so I wanted Moira to ensure you're taken care of during the festivities." This caused a double-take from Anslee, but Moira seemed unfazed by the declaration. What did he mean, that she needed to be taken care of? Did he think her so inexperienced that she wouldn't be able to handle herself? The blood rushed to her cheeks, and she felt sure she was turning a nice peony shade when Avery cut into her thoughts.

"Now don't give me that look. I only asked because I'm sure you've not been to the palace more than once, correct?" Avery said.

"Well, yes, but that doesn't mean—"

"And I wouldn't want you to get lost wandering the palace when I must be attending to the royal family."

"Yes, but—"

"Enough of this! Avery, I thought you said you had discussed this with her?" Moira threw a look at Anslee. "How can you expect me to watch her if she plans on misbehaving the entire time?"

Anslee's jaw dropped. Never had anyone treated her so like a child—even when she was a child! Anslee's past as a roamer was never mentioned in front of Moira or Avery. She hoped Avery never found out about it. But even still... her best friend was a lowly cook. She was a servant. If this was what she wanted, why should she let Moira make her feel so out of place? Why didn't she prepare to meet people who expected her to spend her days lolling about with no real work to do?

Anslee expected Avery to stand up for her at any moment, but he just looked more unhappy by the second.

"Moira, I trusted you to take care of this. Anslee, I'm sorry you find this unnecessary, but trust me when I say I disagree. Perhaps you will get along better if you acquaint yourselves without me." Frowning, he turned on his heel and left. Anslee watched him retreat, speechless. Where was the kind-hearted, considerate man that had won her over with walks in the park and surprise gifts? It was getting harder to ignore this darker side of him that she'd seen flashes of.

"Here, have one of these." Moira thrust another champagne flute into her hand. Was this a peace offering?

"Thank you," she grasped the stem, wondering what had caused this change in friendliness.

Moira glanced over at her. "I'm assuming you'll be more malleable after a glass or two. Most of your kind are."

Her cheeks burned again. Apparently, it was obvious she didn't hail from the same royal lines as the rest of the party attendees, despite Avery introducing her as his fiancée. Anslee ignored the barb. Moira may not like her, but she also made no sign of leaving. Perhaps she was already taking Avery's babysitting comment seriously. "How do you know the rest of these people? Are they also distant relatives?"

Moira seemed surprised by her question. "In a way, yes. I've known most of them my entire life."

"Are they also here for the coronation?"

"Yes."

"Will they also need to be 'watched'?" Her sarcasm fell on deaf ears.

"No."

Well, this conversation was going nowhere. Time to find Avery and try to turn this night around. She downed the rest of her flute and discarded it on the tray of a passing servant. "Great to meet you, but I think I'll go find Avery now."

Moira merely raised her eyebrows, and she had already turned to engage a nearby man in conversation before Anslee was out of earshot. "Scintillating conversation with that one."

Anslee glowered as she walked away. She didn't want to offend Avery's family, but if they all acted like that stuck-up courtier, then she was in for a very difficult night... and marriage.

Again, she found Avery in a corner with his manservant Chance. She smiled to herself as she approached them. It wasn't often that she found nobles who treated their servants as close personal friends. Perhaps she had found a lucky one after all. She paused while a rambunctious group of partygoers jumped in front of her, so neither Chance nor Avery saw her approaching. Where did all these relatives come from? Was she expected to meet them all tonight? She supposed she could forgive Avery for throwing a grand engagement party in her honor. Convinced that was how to salvage the night—by allowing Avery to introduce herself to the rest of his family, and hoping they were better natured than the Moira woman—she pushed through the people in her way, pausing in the throng when she overheard their words.

"It's all prepared and will happen at the coronation." That must be Chance. Anslee stopped to overhear. Did this have something to do with Avery? He had mentioned he'd be working at the coronation.

"No, no. I have Moira watching over her. We'll keep her out of the way, away from the action." Was Avery talking about her?

"But what about the others? Are you sure she'll just sit by?" Chance asked.

"As long as this goes according to plan, we won't have to kill anyone for the throne to be ours."

Anslee gasped, clasping her hand to her mouth. Avery was talking about murder!

"Our people have waited for this day a long time. I'm not sure they can wait much longer."

"They'll have to." Avery's voice had a final ring to it. Anslee debated jumping out and confronting him right now. But in a room full of people she had never met... were they all part of this conspiracy?

"Where is the queen? Surely she should know of this plan?" Chance questioned.

"Hush! She can't know. She'd rip her heart out."

"Your face, my lord," Chance asked tentatively. Anslee imagined he grimaced. In the short time she had known Avery, he always looked meticulously put together. The new scars minting his face were unlike him, even though he had brushed it off. Scars like she had seen on him when he accosted her in her bedroom.

"Her patience isn't wearing thin; it's gone. We move at the coronation." Avery's voice was harsh, and Anslee barely dared to breathe as she processed what she was hearing.

Threats to kill for the crown.

A coup to take over the throne.

A people from another kingdom, lying in wait, and harboring a deception so strong that time had not weathered it.

Avery hadn't been lying when they met so long ago. He was from beyond the walls, out in the Eastern Nation. The same nation whose people had used to live here, in the Dracorian Mountains, and had been kicked from their homeland by her people. Had they been planning revenge all this time?

She held in a gasp. She remembered the night in the woods with Robin, feeling the tiny pinpricks of eyes boring into her skull, calculating her every movement. The same intense gazes followed her now. She turned around, pushing her way through the crowd of people until she found Magda. Small shadows slipped from her heels, pooling against the floor, unnoticed by others.

She found Magda and hung off her arm, panting. "I feel terribly sick, Magda. You must come home with me at once."

Magda brushed her off, already in her cups and unwilling to leave. But Anslee was even more unwilling to leave her one friend here with these monsters. Who knew what would happen? "Magda, I swear to all gods you worship that if we do not leave right now, I will vomit all over this gods-damned floor!" she practically yelled, and the few people around them turned their noses at her before turning around and avoiding her completely. Now she was thankful no one here knew who she was. Let them think her some ill courtier too drunk to stay. Were they all traitors to the crown? She needed to get Magda and leave before Avery learned she had eavesdropped—before he came after her! Magda was speechless for once, and she stumbled after Anslee as she stormed out of the mansion and away from the monster she was going to marry.

29

She was done being a stupid servant. She was done being a stupid nobody. While she had stuck her head in the sand, refusing to see the truth that was right in front of her, danger had crept into her home. She packed Magda and herself into the carriage, shouting at Georgie to hurry up and drive them home. She settled back into the carriage cab and closed her eyes, trying to ignore the events of the last few hours. She dozed off. What was she supposed to do? How could she survive this?

She settled against the corner of the cab, and slept the unfit sleep of the guilty. Guilt for running from Avery, guilt for running to Robin, and guilt for mentally accusing Avery of horrible deeds that seemed so impossible in the daylight. She tossed and turned before flinging upright, suddenly wide awake.

The manor wouldn't be safe. What had she been thinking? Avery would know exactly where she had gone. He could be on his way here right now! How long would it have taken him to realize she had been gone? She couldn't hide here. At least, not as she was—weak and powerless. But there was one way to gain power quickly.

She flung open the carriage door, although the horses hadn't slowed down yet.

"Hey now, where are you off to?" Georgie cried.

"Careful!" Magda shrieked, trying to drag her back into the carriage.

But Anslee leaped and dashed off. "Return home without me!" she cried. They would be safe there. They would have to be. Avery didn't want anything from them. It was her he wanted.

She felt a calling to return to the woods, and as if in a dream, regardless of the hesitation she should have felt, she followed it. She raced through town without passing a single soul. She could have sworn she walked right past Robin's camp, but she heard and saw nothing, and no one appeared suddenly to follow her or try to shoot her. Small blessings, she thought, as her feet moved on without her knowledge.

Shadows pooled on the forest floor. Darkness dripped from the leaves as she passed by, reaching out to touch her. Greenery awoke and unfurled, trailing after her. The crown called to her, although she could not see it. It had been silent when she searched for it before, but now it called out to her in her time of need.

She ran as if in a daze, memories from a previous life mirroring her actions today. She moved past a long-forgotten roamer campsite, barely noticeable to anyone who hadn't been there. Up and down hills until she reached a clearing. The shadows tumbled after themselves in their earnestness to reach her, growing larger the farther they walked. They reached out and tapped her heels, but she paid them no mind. At last, she reached an empty clearing. Moonlight filtered through the trees. Her vision fractured. She momentarily saw the clearing alive with sunlight, dust motes streaming in the air from her ten-year-old viewpoint. She blinked and the inky night enveloped her. Darkness pooled at the edge of the clearing, as if waiting for her. Vines trailed along the ground, passing the invisible barrier and reaching out to her. And suddenly Anslee knew.

The crown had been there all along, waiting for her to find it. Only she could convince the earth to move, as if by magic.

She slid to the ground, wiping her hands tentatively against the earth. Moss and lichen melted away, peeling backward to reveal old and warped tree roots. She couldn't believe what she was seeing. The earth responded to her gentle touch, her call to reveal more of itself.

And suddenly she realized... It was magic. Magic was real. And she had it. Loads of it. She was innately magical, walking around, it sloughed off her like dead skin, and the faintest tendrils that she left behind had turned into these dark shadows that trailed after her like silent little pets. As if realizing they were recognized and understood, these dark darlings—her darklings—streamed forward, covering her legs, splashing against her. And she was unafraid. She bent down, letting them leap and slip off her arms, and bent down at the now visible crown at the roots of a giant tower of a tree.

She reached out a hand tentatively. This was what everyone had been searching for? It looked like it had just been sitting here, waiting to be found. Just like she remembered seeing when she was a small child. As if it had been waiting for her specifically to find it.

Growing bolder, she stretched out her hand and grabbed it, palming one of the large garnet colored bloodstones encircling the gold band. A sharp pain bit into her palm and she dropped it suddenly, yelping. The spell broke. The darklings recoiled.

The crown bounced off the ground and rolled a few feet away. A subtle mark had been branded into her palm. She traced the outline on her hand, savoring the feel of her fingertip against the scarred skin of her lifeline, the same palm that Avery had caressed earlier. It was the mark of the bloodstone. She paused for a moment, but no one came running at her cry. As she had hoped, there was no one around to hear. Who else would be out in the woods?

As a child, the crown had been harmless when she had touched it. But had that even been true? Or another false memory? She hadn't believed in magic then... Maybe her new awareness made her malleable to the crown's desires. But could an inanimate object have desires?

The vines that had been trailing her lifted the crown up to shoulder height, as if the land wanted her to touch it. She gingerly picked up the crown again, but did not feel an echoing bite. For just a moment, she wondered what it would be like to take this crown and place it upon her head. What would it feel like to be a princess, if only for a moment? She trembled with excitement and adrenaline. She knew, of course, that the real purpose of finding this crown was the reward she hoped to achieve. A reward that would have her coasting through the rest of her life with enough money to buy whatever she needed. Starting with a place of her very own. She no longer needed this crown to bring wealth to Avery. She could use it to hide herself. What could it hurt to try on? No one else would ever know.

She stood in a patch of moonlight in the middle of the clearing where she had first stumbled upon this crown. Gingerly, she raised it up and set it down upon her curls. Pain shot forth from every place the metal band touched her skin. She clutched her forehead, screaming and fell to the ground. Nausea flowed through her, and she heaved on the forest floor. Her brain was burning up, like there would be nothing left but cinders. Pain overwhelmed her. And as her mind burned, visions surged into her.

But these memories could not possibly be hers. Looking up at strange faces, changing hands, bright light shining all around her, followed by bright blood. So much blood. The images continued to flash, and she realized she was seeing history from the crown's vantage point. Impossible!

She lay on the ground, face pressed against the damp earth and arms flung out to her sides. It was excruciating painful as the crown continued to bombard her with images. It wanted her to see the awful, horrible things that it had caused! She managed to roll over to her side and agonizingly, she raised her hands up her sides, and yanked off the crown. She lay there, feeling blood slowly trickling down her face. When she could move her fingers, she examined her skull and found nothing. She pulled her fingers away and saw they were clear. Shadows dripped down her fingers. What had this magic done to her?

She did not have the luxury to focus on this non-existent wound though, since the last images the crown had projected into her mind were playing on repeat. The face of a father and mother, smiling at a youngling in a throne room—a youngling that was her. And then, darkness as the babe—as she—was gathered up and whisked away in complete silence. No warning. No sounds. Nothing to indicate the true nature of the attacker. But his face was etched in her memories. She saw it every afternoon. Dreamed about it at night.

It was the face of her betrothed.

30

Anslee awoke in a pool of her own sweat. She was angry.

She had always felt as if she were wanting. Well, turns out it was everyone else who was wanting.

Anslee was the true heir to the power of this land! And there was magic here, to be sure. No matter that Their Majesties had tried to hide it through royal decrees. Even though the people whispered about magic as if it didn't exist... as if it was something to fear. Well, the people should be afraid. This magic was power—her power. And she could finally make those people who had made her feel so bad know what it was like to be subject to her power.

She wasn't sure how much time had passed, but she still lay under the cover of darkness with the firm earth beneath her. So it hadn't been a dream after all. She uncurled from the fetal position, scraping her knee against a dirty crown. No, definitely not a dream. She inspected the metal for hidden supernatural elements, anything that could have caused that storm through her mind. But nothing untoward appeared.

Where to go from here? Leave the crown in the woods, abandoning it, and returning to her bed to forget this ever happened? She had tried that once before, as a child. She knew that memory had been real now. And the other 'memories' the crown had shared with her? What were those? False memories implanted in the crown itself by an unknown mage? Was the crown itself alive? She dropped it and jumped away at the thought.

She heard the rustling of small animals throughout the forest and realized she probably wasn't alone out here. Better to leave quickly, before a larger, wiser animal found her and gobbled her up. She was hesitant to bring the crown with her, despite running deep into the woods to find it. She had been in an uncontrollable stupor, barely containing her own emotions. At least that's how she felt. Powerless. Subject to the whims of this object. All she had ever wanted was a safe corner of the world to call her own. A family to love her and ground her. A crowd to huddle in for safety. But she knew picking this crown up would somehow change everything. She could no longer pretend to be a willful child, deserving of having all her whims catered to. Choosing to handle this royal scion of power meant she would be responsible for something besides her own happiness. Hopefully, it wouldn't ask for much more. It wanted to be picked up.

She scooped the crown up. She tucked it against her right side, wrapped it in the edges of her cloak, and drew the other half of her cloak closer. At first glance, no one would suspect she cradled a secret crown that had the land in a silent uproar for the past twenty years.

She started trudging through the forest. Her fevered state had driven her here, and she had no recollection of how to get back home. At least moving kept her blood pumping and her mind going. Perhaps she would run into Robin and one of his roamers? Or the other, darker shadows that trolled her nightmares could appear. She suppressed the hysterical laughter bubbling inside her. Who knew what to expect? The woods were no place for a young maidservant. Or a betrothed woman to a young Lord.

Or a hidden princess.

Lost in her musings, she didn't notice the whisper of a knocked arrow and the shadow of a person stepping out behind her.

"Stop walking or I'll shoot."

Anslee froze, terrified. Hadn't this been what she expected to happen?

"Hands up, where I can see them. No hiding any weapons." The harsh voice was a woman she recognized. Leaves crunched under her feet as she marched closer.

Anslee giggled maniacally. She wasn't unarmed. Holding onto the crown tighter, aware she was sitting on all this power and Cria did not know! If she knew how to use this power, she could decimate Cria with only a thought. Anslee shrugged her cloak forward. She couldn't let go of the crown! Not like this!

"Anslee? Is that you?" Cria asked.

Anslee whirled around, the crown still clutched tight to her side. "Cria! Am I ever glad to see you!" Someone pressed a dagger against her throat, preventing her from saying anything more.

"She said put your hands up," a voice growled in her ear.

Cria sighed. "Ziter, put your weapon down. I can, unfortunately, vouch for this one." The dagger was swiftly removed from her throat, but a thin line of blood was left, Anslee assumed on purpose. If Cria noticed, she said nothing. She suppressed another manic laugh. She was on the verge of losing control, and who knew what would happen then if she wasn't aware enough to control the crown?

"I assume you want to see *him*, again?" Cria shook her head and turned around, confident they would follow her. "Let's go then. Ziter, stay here and keep watch. The things you get away with... Robin would skin the rest of us for the crap he puts up with from you." Anslee assumed she meant the line of blood that trickled down her neck and over her elaborate gown, a gown that was now ripped and stained, but Cria didn't chastise Ziter any more.

They walked in silence to the roamer camp. Robin didn't seem surprised at her visit, although he couldn't hide the wary look on his face.

"Always a pleasure, Anslee. Cria, if you don't mind?"

Cria rolled her eyes and stomped out, leaving the other two alone in Robin's tent. She hadn't noticed his inner haven last time, and her eyes devoured all the tiny details about his life. The handful of books against a cot in the corner, a large wooden table covered in maps and scrolls and lists. She took a step closer and wondered if one of these scrolls contained a sketch of her bloodstones.

"Enjoy what you see? A far cry from the manors you're used to, I'm sure." He couldn't keep the bitterness out of his voice. He eyed her fancy dress and bloodstone necklace that she wore.

Robin shuffled the papers into a pile, discreetly whisking the blood stone sketch out of her sight. "I'm surprised to see you so soon. Is everything alright?"

He seemed hesitant to get too close to her, without the urgency that had been in his voice the last time they were together. He took in the sparkling gems on her ring finger too.

"I have something for you."

Or at least that's what she tried to say. But the words stuck in her throat. In her mind, she backed away after handing him the crown and ran fast and furious back to her little room atop the manor. She wanted to tell him what she had found. Gods, she wanted to give it to him and wash her hands of this whole bloody episode. But she couldn't.

"Lee, why are you here?" His voice was more forceful this time, grounding her back down to his reality. He looked up at her sharply, and she was a little taken aback at the anger in his voice.

She went on the offensive. "It was your goons who brought me here! If Cria would just leave me alone, we wouldn't have to deal with each other again." She paused. She needed to tell him something. Avery wouldn't stop at her.

"You were right though..." she whispered. "The shadows. The creatures. They are here in the city. They're coming for... us," she finished. She wanted to say they're coming for *me*, but again the words caught in her throat.

"I can't say it's entirely unexpected. We expected as much. They're searching for the crown." His eyes were back on the table. He was avoiding eye contact with her. He didn't want her here.

She fingered the frayed edges of her cape, dirty after her run through the woods, noting where the crown rim had caught against the edges. It kept her from looking at Robin as she answered. "I'm not sure what you mean."

"Lee, you know you do!" Her nickname burst forth from him as it always did in heightened times of passion, and he strode across the room to grip her shoulders. "Look at me! You know you found this once before! I know you remember, Lee. Don't shut down on me now." He barely whispered the last sentence, and her head jerked to the side, as if avoiding his gaze would also block her from hearing him.

He released her and took a step back. "If you can't admit it, then I don't know what help you are to us. Maybe you should leave again." She suspected he knew more than he was letting on. That perhaps he had already known about these visions the crown had shown her. And if that was true, how could she ever trust him?

"What about the crown?" she blurted out. She needed to throw him off her trail if he she couldn't trust him. Could she really escape with the crown this easily?

"Are you out here looking for it?" he asked.

She didn't have an answer for him.

"That's what I thought. Go home, Anslee. We'll take care of it."

She backed slowly away, stealing one last look at Robin before hurrying outside the tent. He didn't move to stop her. He was right. She had wanted to bring the crown here, so someone else could take her problems away from her and deal with them. Robin would do that, as he'd promised the last few weeks—take the crown and the reward that came with it. He only ever wanted her to help find it. And a few days ago, she would have gladly let him, and continued to ignore the political scheme she had woken up to.

But, in the moment of truth, it hadn't felt right to share with him. It was her crown. She had found it. It belonged to her. Her palms gripped its edges, and she looked down to hide her grin. She hadn't meant to steal away from the woods with a hidden crown. Was relieved that Robin hadn't suspected. Holding it, she knew it wasn't meant for just anyone.

It was meant for her.

31

The violent wind she had been fighting on her way out of the city had turned into a torrential downpour right before Anslee stepped inside. She needed to ease her way upstairs without knocking anything over or causing any noise that would awaken the household. She slowly turned back around and jumped backward as a flash of lighting and thunder illuminated the outline of a person suddenly standing in the doorframe between the kitchen and the hallway.

Another flash of the lighting and she saw it was Magda, standing there with a rolling pin clenched between her fingers, ready to wreak havoc like the gods themselves. Anslee sagged against the door behind her.

"Gods, Magda, you gave me a fright!" she whispered across the room.

The other woman folded her arms across her chest, rolling pin drooping downwards. "Don't tell me you're over your fear already. Where the gods have you been? You gave me a fright jumping out of the carriage like that! Poor Georgie has run off to find the constable to bring you home!" Despite her anger, she was still keeping her voice quiet. Normally, Magda yelled until she was blue in the face if something angered her that much. They had learned long ago the man they served slept like the dead, and would not wake for a little thing like some loud verbal chastisement. "Lucky I realized you had let yourself out before alarming our guest."

The color drained for the second time that night. There would only be one person here this late to see her. One person wanting to know why she ran from his party.

Avery.

"Yes, that's right. Who else?" Magda snapped back. Anslee hadn't realized she had whispered his name aloud.

"Is… is he still here?" she stuttered.

"Of course he's still here," Magda snapped back at her. "He's refused to leave until he sees you, even though I've insisted you're sleeping and exhausted from the party." She stepped back to get a good look at Anslee and tsk-ed at her. "At least you've kept out of the rain. Now hurry and prepare to say hello to him. We can say I've just woken you, but he must leave. Quick, get out of that ruined dress and into these clothes." Tactfully, she said nothing about the dirt Anslee had tramped into the kitchen. Wordlessly, Magda took her coat and clothes and shoved them in a corner, and handed her a nightdress and robe. In the shuffle, Anslee took the crown and shoved it under the tulle skirt of her ruined ball gown, relieved Magda did not see.

She followed Magda as she slipped down the hall and into the parlor, where Magda shooed her to enter. Avery must be waiting in here. She paused for a moment, gathering her thoughts. If Avery truly was behind this *coup…* No, she could not afford to think about this. She opened the door and slipped through. Avery was indeed waiting for her inside, and jumped up from lounging against the couch once she entered. He opened his arms for her to obediently walk into, but she kept her distance. He did not appear concerned at her sudden appearance.

His arm dropped back down to his side, and he stiffened as her scent wafted over to him. "You smell like the forest and air heavy with the promise of rain," he murmured.

"I like to sleep with my windows open. I was told you wanted to see me?" The lie came easily to her lips, in contrast to the rigid tension held in her body.

He took a step closer, gently taking her hand in both of his. If he were to look down, her muddy slippers would give away her lies.

Anslee mentally checked herself from jerking them back to her side. She could give him no reason to question her. He cocked his head while he stared at her, calculating. He did not believe she had been asleep upstairs, she could tell, but he also could not confidently say where else she might have been.

How had she never noticed how predatory that grin was before? Or maybe she had, but his carefully calculated disguise as a member of the gentry had fooled her.

His persona was meticulously formulated to entice and to lure, but not to love. No, never to love. He must have noticed the change in her expression, for he suddenly frowned.

"Is everything all right, my sweet?" His hands squeezed hers painfully.

"I awoke from a nightmare," she told him, not knowing where the lies came from that spewed from her mouth. Perhaps because she felt like she was living them. "And I came down here to relax when Magda told me you had been waiting for me. Perhaps something seems wrong to you, my lord. Else wise, I do not know why you are here at this late hour?"

"What were your nightmares about?" he challenged her softly. She knew he was fishing for information. At least this part she did not have to make up. She may not have had them tonight, but they had been regular occurrences these past few weeks. Her eyelids lowered to cover her eyes, and she stared at the floor, the dark images sweeping through her.

"Of darkness," she whispered. "Of creatures that should not exist turning real, and chasing me through dark forests and city streets, but then turning into smoke when I turn to face them." She had not realized how true that was until she spoke the words. Her nightmares had been a jumbling of recurring images—faces she had not remembered seeing, snatches of sentences she had not remembered hearing, but always that dark evil swirling slowly closer and the smoke from the flames threatening to devour her. Pour into her lungs until she was nothing more than a glass vessel for the evil darkness to thrive in—and then shatter. They would break her, like she had broken that glass vase in Crio's tent those weeks ago.

Avery must have watched her emotions play against her face. He saw the horror and dread that she had not been able to properly describe. He rubbed his hands over her arms one last time. His own dark eyes turned into inky pits of blackness and she could tell he was deeply angered, although over what she was unsure. Certainly not her nightmares. Perhaps he knew what had been causing them in the first place. If her visions tonight had been true, then she would have thought Avery would be the one causing those nightmares in the first place. It looked like that, at least, was not true. His hands fell away, but he had one last reassurance to give her.

"Go back to sleep, my sweet. And rest easy knowing that I will keep watch over you." She should have felt comforted over his words, but all she felt was dread.

She resolved to leave him, leave this city, leave this life. *It's better to start out as a roamer far, far away where no one knows me than live a single other instant here, knowing what I now know*, she thought.

He must have seen the disbelief in her face. He sneered. "So we're dropping the charade then?" he asked.

She stared at him.

"I believe you have something of mine."

She backed away, "No, never."

"Don't stall for time. It's unlike you, princess," he said harshly.

She gasped. What was he implying? Certainly not that her visions had been true.

"Oh come now, you must have put it all together. You're not some roamer throwaway. You come from royalty. Why, even the plants of the land recognize this and reach for you. Did you think I wouldn't notice? Did you think no one would notice?" He laughed, but it wasn't the jovial chuckle she expected from him. No, his laugh was enmeshed in cruelty and haughtiness.

He darted forward, quick as a whip, and pulled the crown from Magda's unsuspecting hands. She had been hiding in the corner. Must have gotten curious after all, and pulled the crown from Anslee's ruined gowns. Anslee lunged at him, but he swatted her away. She was no match for his strength.

"All that fuss for this gaudy thing?" he asked, holding up the clunky gold and ruby encrusted crown. "Although... it looks like they replaced these rubies with bloodstones." He guffawed.

"Now does it all make sense, my princess?" He saw the wheels turning, coming together... "No matter. You are mine now." He smiled wickedly. He snapped his fingers and chains appeared around Anslee's arms and legs. She gasped, jerked backward, and promptly tripped over her own feet and fell in a tangled heap.

"And before you even think of screaming..." He stepped closer and bent down to her level. She lunged for him, forgetting her arms were trapped and he backhanded her. She flew across the room, smacking into the wall and sliding back down to the ground.

"You are mine now, princess," he growled.

The room rippled, and she sank into unconsciousness.

32

She awoke in a dungeon.

Anslee had never been in a dungeon before. At least, she assumed that's where she was. Cold, damp stones beneath her body. A cot in the corner, although no one had placed her on it. Shackles still chained her ankles and wrists. What would happen to her now?

What about Magda and Georgie? Would they go looking for her? Would he target her as well?

She curled up in a ball, hugging herself tight and buried her head.

Had Robin suspected she had the crown? That she brought it into their camp and hid it right under their noses? They could have easily taken it from her, just as Avery had done. Had they known? Or had Robin suspected and let her keep it, anyway? He had kept his promise to stay away... it had been his guards who found her and brought her to him. She had been lost in the woods. Anslee sobbed harder. She couldn't even be a roamer right anymore. Getting lost in her own woods—what was wrong with her?

But then, if what Avery had said was true... Then she shouldn't have needed anyone's help. She should never have gotten lost. She should have been able to find her own way out.

If she was really one with the land... what did that even mean? And what did the crown have to do with all of this?

Her mind jumped back to the roamers. To Magda, worried for her. To Georgie, running as fast as he could to get help. To the unsuspecting neighbors that didn't realize a monster lived beside them. Who would care about them? Who would help those people?

Her mind couldn't keep a straight thought.

Her head still burned from touching the crown.

But maybe what Avery said was true, and she had a connection with the land. Then didn't she owe it to those people to protect them?

Someone had lied to them, their whole lives. Told them that magic didn't exist. That if it did, it must be dangerous. That no one outside the borders could be trusted. Well, at least that last part was right. But why had they been told that? What secrets were the Dracor rulers hiding?

She wouldn't put her head in the sand any longer. She was done hiding who she was and what she could do.

Avery had called her a princess? A power to be reckoned with?

Well, he can see what sort of power she could be.

33

Anslee tried calling little animals. Chipmunks, birds, squirrels, raccoons. No one came. Apparently, Anslee wasn't that sort of princess. Her so-called innate connection with the land was limited to just that—the land. Animals paid her no mind.

Anslee held out her hand, and a spot of darkness trickled down from the open window to land on her palm. She had these, at least. Although she still wasn't exactly sure what these were. She had finally convinced herself they weren't shadows. They were too solid to be a trick of the light.

Heavy footsteps approached. She put her hand behind her back, and let her mysterious sidekick trickle off.

"At last, my betrothed. How far you have fallen." White teeth gleamed in the darkness, sharp and fierce. A predator's teeth.

"Who are you?" Anslee asked.

He flashed a grin. "Avery Varrock, of course, Lord of the Eastern Whilliswoods." He was testing her. His eyes gleamed in the darkness. Anslee curled in on herself. He grinned wider, as if that's the sort of prey instinct he was hoping to draw out.

"Surely that's not all," Anslee said, full of a bravado she did not really feel. "If I am really a princess." Anslee drew the word out sarcastically. No one was playing now. Anslee raised her arm and shook her chains, as if to emphasize her point. "Then you are really...?" Anslee let the question drift off and linger between them.

"At long last," he breathed. Was he happy now? "You understand the game." A shiver coursed up her spine.

Had our engagement, our courting, our getting to know one another all been a game to him? Had he been toying with me all this time?

He apprised her, rocking back on his heels and clasping his hands in front of him. "Oh, go on and take your time. I can see the wheels in there spinning... slowly, but spinning nonetheless. Must take a while to get started since they've been standing still for so long." And just like that her wheels, as he so eloquently put it, came to a crashing halt.

"You're one of them. The ones kicked out of this land eons ago! The creatures that have been harassing and killing the citizens ever since the princess returned..."

"Ah yes, and the rest of that realization would be..."

"That she's one of you too. That you're putting a pretender on the throne. And came here to kill us for revenge!"

"Oh, Anslee," he sighed. "And just when I thought I had high hopes for you. No, my sweet, poor child. We're not here for revenge. Well, maybe she is. She can have quite the temper." His laugh turned sour, and Anslee remembered the half-healed scars she had seen on his face more than once.

"We're here for the power, my dear. For the land. Removing you was the first step in enacting our plan. We scoped the playing field, have been leveling it ever since your ancestors stole it from us, and removing you was simple enough to do. Of course, we never expected for you to survive." He barked out a short laugh. "Or find you back here, of all places. But then you were so conveniently placed for me to find... And so easy to manipulate." He leaned closer to the bars, pressing his cheek against them and reaching forward to caress her cheek. "Tell me," he whispered, his voice a mere breath. "Did it feel real to you?"

Anslee jerked back. Her chains rattled. He laughed and withdrew. "Enough of that. I had one expectation of you, and after a few false starts, I see you have risen to my expectations beautifully."

"The crown," Anslee whispered. There were so many questions she had for him. Why was she not supposed to survive? Had he really been the one trying to dispose of her all those years ago or had the crown's vision lied? Then why had he let her live...?

"Oh yes, the crown. You see, what my queen really needs to seal herself as one with the power of this land, is the magic of the crown. And not just any crown... the one forged in the fires beneath the earth, far under this land, tied to every bit of rock, stone and earth that lives here. To every green thing that grows here. To scrape every morsel of that magic she needs to tie herself wholly to it. And now, thanks to you, that can be achieved during her very coronation ceremony. So really, Anslee must be thanking you, Anslee Marleigh Dracor."

Anslee drew back into her cell, but her back pressed against the cold stone walls. It was the first she had ever heard her name without the unofficial surname of an orphan attached to it. Anslee was now Dracor. Avery dipped into an extravagant bow, the tips of his long hair barely brushing the floor. "Without you, none of this would be possible."

He whirled and slipped out, leaving her alone with her thoughts. Had she really been so foolish? Thinking he had loved her, that they wanted the same things all along. In reality, he had been dropping hints since the moment they first met, claiming her friendship was enough, his eagerness to have her fortune read, even warning her of the people from the east on their first date through the park! And Anslee had lapped it all up, eager for any scrap or morsel of friendliness from him. Oh, he had played her for a fool!

Anslee reached her hand behind her and unfurled her palm, gently inviting the darkling back into her possession. Anslee raised it to her face, and it surprised her that her cheek was wet with tears. Tears of anger.

"My darkling, I have a message for you to take. Avery was foolish, but we have our own allies he knows nothing about. And it's time for us to take control of the magic of the land, and warn them..."

For the first time, Anslee noticed tiny green shoots breaking through the cold ground at her feet. Had those been there before and had Avery failed to realize it? Or did it take her accepting the fact that she might not be powerless for the land to respond to her? She nudged a sprout with her toe, and a flower budded and unfurled. Perhaps she had been the block all along? A low, barely noticeable olive-tinged fog rolled over her feet, and for once, Anslee was not afraid. She thought back to when she had seen it before... during the shadow beast's attack, and again during the verbal onslaught in the woods. Almost as if it had not been there to attack, but to protect her... as if she had unknowingly called forth this green magic of the land to defend her. And here it was again. For the first time, Anslee felt as if she had thrown off the veil covering her eyes and was seeing clearly.

Avery wasn't the only player on the board anymore.

34

"One last time, are you confident in your plans for the day, dear?"

Anslee rolled her eyes. She may be rid of her irons, but she was still shackled to this man. "Enter the palace with you and Moira, sit with Moira and wait while you go off to do... what will you be doing?"

"Tsk, tsk... I'm questioning you, not the other way around."

"Fine, wait while you go off and do *whatever it is you do,* smile politely and clap during the ceremony, stand politely during the after-party ceremony, and finally be taken home after this long, grueling day. Where I will return to my nice, pleasant dungeon."

Anslee had reached an uneasy truce with her feelings for Avery. She could speak with him, but only be compartmentalizing her knowledge that he had stolen her and tricked her and manipulated her... Tiny pin-pricks of pain brought her back to herself, and she uncurled her fingers to reveal half-moon imprints in her palms. Only by squishing those thoughts deep down could she stand to interact with him.

Her anger reignited her throbbing headache, no doubt stress-induced in anticipation of the coronation festivities. And of course, from spending the last few weeks trapped in a dungeon. Her headache worsened with each of Avery's questions.

"Why darling, you make the day sound positively droll. Don't you agree, Moira?" Avery gave his omni-present grin, but Moira sat stiffly, preoccupied with gazing out the window. He had bargained Anslee's cooperation with the threat of harm to Magda and Georgie. After everything Magda had done for her, Anslee would agree to anything to keep her safe.

Moira spared Anslee a side-eyed glare before returning to gaze out the window. "Of course, she does. She always does. I can't imagine why you put up with her droll attitude, Avery." Anslee would have been offended if she hadn't experienced Moira's attitude throughout the last several weeks. Now the comments rolled off her. Avery countered her argument with how exquisite and enlightening Anslee was and the two continued to make unpleasant small talk until the carriage rolled to a stop.

"Do you ever tire of it?" Anslee snapped, staring at her betrothed.

His smile was predatory. "Tired of what, my dear?"

She waved her hands. "These little games you're playing. You think our lives—my life— is yours for the taking! I'm a person with feelings and goals! I shouldn't be trapped-"

"You will not say a single word more." Suddenly he was in front of her, his eyes glowing and growling at her. "I agreed to bring you on this little endeavor because I thought getting out of that dungeon would be good for you. Because I don't want you escaping again. But if you try to escape or reference your less-than-ideal circumstances outside this carriage..." He gripped her arms painfully and pulled her to him. Talons pressed into the tender skin of her inner wrists. Anslee hissed in pain, but her thoughts went to Magda and Georgie. How much worse would they endure? "You will regret it," he hissed out.

Moira watched with deadened eyes, making no move to interfere.

"And here is where I leave you, my dears." Avery leaned back and pleasantly bowed over their hands, as if the last few moments hadn't happened, before flinging open the carriage doors. Anslee looked down to see a thin line of blood trickling from where he had grabbed her. She pulled her sleeves forward to cover the wound, she didn't want him to notice and make him angrier. They had purposefully given her a dress with loose flowy sleeves to hide the inflamed redness of her wrists, another side effect of all that time in the dungeon.

"Where are you going? Don't leave me here with her!" Anslee lunged after Avery's retreating back, but he never stopped to turn around. He left her with Moira, and Anslee's arms drooped as she realized he had abandoned her with the she-demon. She had hoped that was Avery's bravado talking. He, at least, she understood, and had a better chance of escaping. She hadn't anticipated being stuck with Moira, and hoped the last minute change wouldn't interfere with other plans she had set in motion.

"That was unexpected. He never gives such displays of affection, especially in public, especially to a human." Moira arched an eyebrow in surprise. "Peculiar. But for some reason, he worries about you. Come along then, I suppose you're lost in such luxury again."

Had Moira been paying attention at all? That was not a display of affection. Anslee wondered what was wrong with Moira. Were all of these eastern creatures so cold and cruel, indifferent to understanding complex human emotions? And what had been with the mention of humans. Were Avery and Moira something other?

Anslee scowled but followed the other woman through the palace. It seemed like it had been ages since she had last been in the palace, but it surprised her to realize it had only been a few months since that fateful night Avery found her. The palace had seemed so surprising and hopeful, the night full of possibilities, but she supposed that was only her projecting her own desires onto the night. Today they walked through large, mazelike corridors, drafty despite their finery. Shadows lurked in the corners, piling on themselves until they looked impossibly high, ready to tip over and devour the crowd of onlookers that had come for the coronation. These weren't her darklings. Has no one else noticed this? What other foul magic was afoot in the palace?

She looked to Moira, but even she didn't notice her shadowy brethren locked into the corners. Was this something only Anslee could see? Was she indeed losing her mind? Perhaps she had been incorrect in judging the need to have someone walk her through this. The palace was much larger than the parts she had originally seen, and surely she would have gotten lost in this throng if she had not been following Moira. She wondered again at the reference to humans, and slowly a memory surfaced of Magda alluding to magical humanoid beings during one of her stories... what had she called them? Moira pushed her forward, and Anslee nearly tripped before hiking up her skirt. It hung loose on her thinner frame.

Where had Avery run off to? And when would this ceremony begin? She would only get one chance to escape.

They finally walked through the Great Hall they had entered for the ball what felt like eons ago. What had once been lively giant plants hanging from the wall and the ceiling had shriveled and died. They were a pale imitation of what they once were. New potted plants, evil looking with curled blood red leaves had been imported into the Great Hall, and now lined the walkway. They looked ready to reach out and snap the guests. Anslee kept her hands to herself. This was a far cry from the lively greenroom they had walked through before. No doubt another influence of the false princess.

Moira ushered her through the crowd and to designated seats in the room's front. At her smirk, Anslee scowled. She heard her chains clank with every step, even though she wore no irons. The sound haunted her, even here.

"What's so funny?"

"How unobservant you little humans are, my dear. Look around. You are surrounded." Anslee took the time to really look at the other guests and she gasped when she noticed what she thought were Avery's unique features—flawless skin, an air of haughty refinement, sharp eyes, muscular builds. She was surrounded by women and men that were too beautiful to exist. At her gasp, several pairs of bright eyes turned to glare at her. She cowered into Moira's skirts, who pulled her along with a little tug.

Fae.

That's what Magda had called them. That's what this crowd was largely composed of. The vast majority of people weren't human like her.

Moira's smirk grew into a full-fledged satisfied smile. "These are our warriors," the fae whispered into Anslee's ear, pulling her into a seat amidst them. "As you can tell, we came prepared for any contingencies. So don't get any ideas, little princess." The last words were a whisper upon her ear, and Anslee couldn't be certain she had heard correctly. Did everyone know the truth about her?

Trumpets blared, and as one, the beautiful creatures turned to look. Anslee jumped up from the seats they had been given. There was a fierce pain in her mind that filled her with such anxiety and dread, she didn't know how she could sit there and do nothing. Where was this feeling coming from?

"Sit down," Moira hissed and yanked on her skirt, almost toppling Anslee as she moved away. Her mind scrambled for an excuse to leave. The humans near them turned to glare and shush them.

"I just have to use the ladies' room. Too much punch beforehand and all that." Anslee scampered two seats further away.

"It's about to start! Get back here!" Moira reached out a clawed hand, but Anslee let loose a young red sapling she had snagged on their way walking into the palace. With a thought, it sprouted and tied Moira's slippers to her seat. At the loud screeching noise that ensued from the chair being dragged forth, humans and fae alike turned to glare and reprimand Moira. She cowed as the monarchs entered the far end of the Great Hall.

"I'll be right back," Anslee whispered, already down the aisle and sprinting away. But she wouldn't be. Her head shrieked, urging her on. Others were turning to look at her and she knew then Moira wouldn't follow her. She couldn't bear to make a scene, especially, since she suspected that was the whole reason Avery had insisted that she join them in the first place. For Anslee had finally placed the headache raging within her. The crown was calling her.

35

Anslee staggered down a side hallway, barely avoiding running into enlightened royals, ladies, and lords making their own way to their seats. Was this why Moira had wanted to find their seats so early? To trap her in this audience? She slumped against the wall as another wave of anxiety and dread filled her. The crowd paid her no heed as it rushed past. She had to keep going, find what was causing this if only to put a stop to her own aching head. She pushed her way through the crowd, letting her pounding head drive her. Great gasps of air diminished the need to vomit. She turned down a deserted side corridor. She couldn't take the pain anymore. The cold stone felt nice pressed against her feverish forehead. The pain reached insurmountable levels as she crept closer to a sturdy oak door embellished with crawling vines and plants. She had wanted to escape during the coronation, not stay trapped within the palace! But she couldn't move any farther for the pain. She reached her hand out to open the door.

She stumbled, literally, into an almost unbelievable scene.

A woman identical to her lounged on a dais against a backdrop of windows, beside a pedestal that housed a golden crown. A replica of the crown that Anslee had found in the woods. Light streamed through the windows, highlighting the woman's shimmery gown, but shadowing her expression. And beside this woman stood Avery, who looked just as shocked to see her, for once. Across the room, holding another golden crown, was Robin. She looked back and forth in astonishment. To see Avery with a royal, preparing for the coronation, wasn't all that much of a surprise. He had basically told her that's all he'd be doing today... But to see that this woman did indeed look like her doppelgänger was a shock. And to see Robin here as well? She was glad her warning had reached him.

"What the gods?" she wheezed out, leaning against the wall as another wave of nausea overtook her.

"Avery, I thought you promised you had dealt with her?" The clear high-pitched voice could only come from the woman against the wall. She looked like a fairy-tale princess, and Anslee suddenly realized that's exactly what she was. All those stories Robin had told her, of a hidden danger stalking this nation's denizens, of Magda's stories of a hidden crown and a hidden princess, of overhearing Avery speaking of a coup, and even of her own suppressed memories that revealed themselves in dreams and visions. This image of the woman before her, hair floating around her on wisps of air, raising her hand that cackled with long-forgotten magic, was an imposter. Her imposter. And she had planned to peacefully take this kingdom, without force, and hold it again for her own people. Anslee slumped to the ground, overcome with her own stupidity in ignoring all the signs her mind had slowly been counting. And now it was over. She had lost without ever trying, outmaneuvered in this battle.

"What a pity she's still alive. I had assumed you had disposed of her, or at least better hidden her. I certainly never expected to see you here, on *my* coronation day." The faux princess barely sounded perturbed. "I suppose I'll just have to finish you myself, since no one else could be bothered to do it."

Avery stepped in front of his future Queen, gripping his sword's hilt. "Are you sure that is wise, my queen?" he asked with a short bow, surprising them all.

The princess—no, the fae queen—sneered at him, raising a hand to let golden magic drip down her arms and sizzle where it touched the floor.

"Have you become so fond of this creature that first you lie to me, and then you rush to defend her?" she asked.

Before Avery could answer, Robin jumped in front of Anslee, drawing his own sword. Where had that come from? Anslee grimaced. These men couldn't let her fight her own battles. The queen laughed as if she too recognized their babying.

"Two men protecting the poor forgotten princess?" she sneered. "Guess what, boys. I don't think she wants to be rescued." For the first time since Anslee entered, the Queen rose gracefully from her chair and strode down the dais toward them. Avery tracked her movements, now crouched in a fighting stance. She ignored him, and when Robin drew back his arm to attack, she simply flung her fingers in his direction and he flew across the room. Golden magic splattered around him and Anslee winced at his cry of pain.

A hazy aura settled around the imposter princess from her magic use, shadowy and hazy. The only thing Anslee could see of her was her golden outline where the magic glowed. Anslee gasped and scrambled to her feet to run to Robin, but the fae princess was already in front of her, pressing her backward with every step she took. It was disconcerting, looking into a face eerily similar to her own, the rest of the body hidden by shadows.

"What are you waiting for dear? The crown is yours, the throne is yours. If you want it..." The princess's face, so eerily similar to her own, glared at her. She gestured at the crown still atop the pedestal. Anslee glared back but made no move forward. Truthfully, she had never considered this far ahead in all of her planning. Did she even want to be the next queen? Leave her comfortable life to take on the responsibility of leading a nation? All she ever wanted was to belong somewhere. But a small belonging—to matter to her family, to a life partner. Did she want to belong to a whole country? Could she be a hero? She took a hesitant step forward, wavering in her commitment, and felt her steps slow, as if she was walking in molasses.

The Future Queen of the Dracorian Mountains crowed her glee. "The little sparrow finally moves! But you did not think I would make this easy for you, did you little sparrow?" Anslee grunted with the effort but kept pushing forward through the magic. Shadows gathered behind her, more and more, as if all the hidden darkness in the palace had surged forward to overcome her. She cried out, but no, the shadows were helping her. They were pushing her forward, pressing against her, impossibly strong and supportive. Olive-tinged wisps trailed around her—the magic of the land, that elusive olive-green fog that helped her on occasion, and was here now, supporting her claim. The sight of the magic strengthened her, and she pushed forward with all the fear she had felt at Avery locking her in the dungeon, with all the worry she felt for Magda and Georgie and Robin, with all her frustration at lack of controlling her own future. She gathered her resolve together and *pushed*. The magic gave an inch beneath her fingertips. She felt like the magic would squeeze her between the wall of shadows at her back and the invisible magical barrier to her front.

The queen was a few tantalizing steps out of reach, an ever-moving target. She frowned, as if noticing that something was not quite right. The surrounding air grew ever hazier with her enemy's magic use.

"My crown!" the Queen demanded, flinging an arm out.

Avery wavered, and the slight hesitation caused her face to mottle purple and red with rage.

She heard the taut bowstring of an arrow released in flight. A sweet song from childhood. She had forgotten about Robin, and apparently he had taken a stand where he fell and played to his strengths. She kept pushing while the arrow flew forward. Robin never missed.

The queen cackled again, grabbed the arrow out of the air with her clawed fingertips. When did those claws appear? Anslee *pushed* another few inches forward. The shadowy horde behind her was crushing her. They were insistent.

Win. Win. Win, they chanted.

Take. Take. Take.

Avery strode forward with the crown, the true crown, in his hand. The one that he had stolen from Anslee, and she felt the magic emanating from it in waves. How had she never noticed that before? If the faux princess touched it, then surely something terrible would happen. She couldn't let her have it. It was her or them. But she also couldn't reach her in time. She strained, gaining another few inches.

The faux princess reached for the crown, fingers outstretched. Another twang, and she whirled, talons ready. But Robin had aimed for her dress, and Anslee stuck to the ground, unable to step forward. Avery stopped walking, hesitating, looking between the two potential princesses of the human land.

The Queen screeched her frustration, ripping the arrow from her gown and throwing it back at Robin. Robin slid back to the wall, his shoulder struck. Blood poured from it. His face whitened, and he gripped his shoulder with his hand. How strong she must be to strike him without a bow!

"The crown is mine!" she roared, lunging forward.

Anslee had been edging ever closer. The shadows piled impossibly high behind her, eclipsing any light that entered the room. Anyone who looked in would see only a wall of writhing green opaqueness. She screamed her frustration—the crown was *right there*, but she still felt so far away.

Beyond her, Avery turned at her scream and his eyes widened, as if he at last saw the power of the land behind her, supporting her claim to the crown. He drew his sword in his free hand.

Claim. Claim. Claim.

More arrow strings twanged. At this range Robin couldn't miss. But they had forgotten about the Queen's magic. Long-stemmed flowers fell harmlessly to the ground where arrows should have struck true.

"It's the crown!" Robin shouted at Anslee, still stuck to the wall behind her. "It must be tied to the land's magic. They can't complete their ritual without it! Grab it and run!"

The whispers were in her mind, driving her crazy, toying with her sanity. It was all she could feel. Darkness narrowed her vision. It was all she could see. With a final push, she tore free from the magic, lunging for the queen. The scars from her wrists broke free, and blood streamed after her, mixing with the shadows that still tailed her. She knocked the queen to the ground, and she roared. It was a messy fight. Anslee wasn't trained in any military style and neither appeared the queen. She sliced at Anslee's stomach, and Anslee punched her in the nose. Blood streamed down her face. Must be broken. The queen tried to pluck the inside of Anslee's intestines open, but she crawled over her, trapping her body, pulling her hair, elbowing her in the face again. She reached for the crown that Avery still held. They had rolled to his boots. He stared down at them, emotionless. She pulled the crown from his fingers, and he didn't stop her. Was it a trap? No time to wonder now.

The crown reached back for her. She felt it now. Like the elements of nature behind her, pushing her to reach forward to grab it, the crown wanted her to take it. It wanted to be in her hands. All the fear and shame she had felt hiding from her past as a roamer blazed within her. Anslee rode the shame like a wave of recognition, making it hers. She hadn't spent her childhood playing in the mud and being shunned from town to town. She had been connecting with the land, soothing it, cultivating the land's power and preparing to take the place that had always belonged to her.

Light blazed forth where Anslee touched the crown. The Queen screamed. The parts of her visible in the golden hazy light burned. Anslee rolled off her, the crown gripped in her hands, bloody and sharp.

The half-charred queen raised herself on one elbow, gathering her legs under her and preparing to attack.

What to do? Anslee had captured the crown, but she didn't know how to use its power. She didn't know how to protect herself. She gripped it in both hands, crouching low. She'd bang the damn thing over the woman's head and crush her with it. She vowed to use every source of strength at her disposal.

But she had forgotten about Avery, and as the queen lunged, Anslee whirled and grabbed Avery's sword, and with a hefty swing cut a bloody slash through the Queen. She bled from left shoulder to navel. Anslee would run for freedom. To save this kingdom. And to save herself.

The Queen grabbed her torso with her hands, as if to staunch the blood. Her face paled and turned sour as she realized the damage. With her last strength, she lunged for the crown from Anslee's grasp, but Avery grabbed a dagger from his boot top and plunged it through the Queen's heart.

An arrow cluttered uselessly to the ground. Anslee hesitantly stepped forward. The crown stopped glowing, and the darkness melted and mewled around her feet. An arrow clattered to the ground. Robin came running. He had pulled out the arrow embedding him to the wall, and he ignored the blood staining his doublet.

Blood gurgled out of the queen's mouth as Avery caught her falling body and lowered her to the floor. She gazed at Avery with her final breath, and her fury turned to shock and sadness. "You..." she wheezed out, "I trusted you." And then she took her last breath and said no more.

Anslee stared down at his forsaken queen. The crown hung uselessly at her side. She had run over before Robin got to her and he came to stand beside her.

"She's dead," Avery stated, his voice void of emotion.

"Of course she is! You stabbed her in the chest!" Robin exploded.

"The heart," Avery corrected, turning black eyes void of grief on them. "It was the only way to stop her." Not *them*, Anslee noted. Avery was staring right at her. Slowly he lowered to one knee, and placing his hands to either side of his knee he bowed his head. "And now I swear my fealty to you, my lady. The one and true princess. May I serve you faithfully and loyally all my days."

"What the gods is wrong with you," Robin snarled, kicking him until he scrambled back to his feet. "Don't we have bigger problems to worry about? And how can you say that? The last person you swore your allegiance to is dead on the ground, by your own hand!" He gestured toward Anslee, and she realized vaguely that the two of them were talking about her. She was still focusing on the dead queen. Would she have been a good ruler? Better than Anslee? She had been condescending and cruel, but she had wanted to rule. The weight of the crown grew heavy in her hand. What would have happened if they had put the crown on her? They'd never know now.

"We can't prove she's an imposter anymore." At her own words, both men stopped their bickering and turned towards her.

"Of course we can. I've known all along. I'll just reveal the truth to the king and queen. After all, I was the one that 'discovered' her and brought her home." Avery's words were full of his usual arrogance, and she wondered how she had never noticed it before.

"You were the... you what?" Apparently Robin was feeling enough emotions for them both. She just felt numb. She tried to focus on their next steps.

"No, that won't work, Avery. We'll all be thrown in the dungeon or killed. They'll never believe us." Her voice sounded far away to her own ears. Remote. Where did they belong now?

"I am not going into a dungeon for you." Robin glared at Avery.

"I don't see why you people are so narrow-minded—"

"Because you killed a woman, Avery! You killed her without provocation, and now we've murdered her and can't prove she was an imposter!" The shouted words surprised even Anslee, and she took a step back to distance herself from her own outburst.

"If no one will believe me, then I suggest we leave," Avery said after a pause.

"How can we trust you? You could set us up for another attack." Robin placed a protective arm around Anslee's shoulders. She barely noticed.

"I've already sworn to protect her, and she's suffering from the numbing effect, a residue left over from battling the queen's magic. We need to get her out of here."

Robin sighed. "At least I can agree with that. I'm not letting her get blamed for a crime you committed." He scooped Anslee up in his arms, and she burrowed into his chest, clutching the crown into her stomach. "Come on Anslee, let's get you home." No, she thought. Not her home. Technically, this palace and everything in it should be her home. They were leaving here, and taking with them their only insurance for a safe return, if they could find out how to leverage it.

No one noticed the shadows stirring in the corners of the room, reaching out as if to follow their would-be heir. Tendrils of darkness raised higher, growing faint and dissipating once they reached the bright noon sunlight streaming through the window. They hissed as the light burned them away.

Epilogue

The three travelers had settled into a familiar pattern by the time the spring rains came. They never stayed in one spot longer than a few days. They rarely spoke to one another. The woman traveling with them was oddly protective of her lone bag of belongings.

The innkeeper watched them prepare to take their leave. They all looked like they could use a strong scrubbing, and they made him feel uneasy. He was glad they had only purchased rooms for a single night.

"How many days ride to the Eastern Whillies?" the tall, dark-haired man asked.

"Haven't you noticed the hazy air? Shorter days? Constant fog?" the innkeeper asked incredulously. "You're already here."

"Impossible," the tall man said, haughty as usual. "I know exactly what the border looks like."

"No one knows that anymore. It creeps closer by the day," the surly innkeeper told them.

The man with wavy brown hair opened his mouth to complain, but shut it after a quick kick in the shins by the young woman. Instead, the three travelers made silent conversation with their eyes, before tipping the innkeeper and walking off into the dense fog.

Acknowledgements

Thank you to my husband, who always supported my dreams of being an author and never made me feel silly for wanting the unreachable. And to my sweet baby boy – who made finding time to write so much harder, but made life infinitely more meaningful.

Thank you to my sisters, who heard about this story a million times, read it half a million, and talked to me about plot holes and characters arcs even more than that. I never would have gotten this far without you.

Thank you to my partner in crime, Jillian Witt, for letting me convince you to try NaNoWriMo one year.

And finally, thank you to my Uncle Bill, who grew up supporting me and showed me you could make a living as an artist.

About the Author

K.E. Blair is an avid reader and lover of all types of fantasy books – YA, NA, urban fantasy, romantic fantasy, epic fantasy, dark fantasy and fairy tales. She writes to escape the mundane and capture the essence of transformation in mythical settings.

You can find her at home curled up with a good book, her dog and her husband, or chasing her toddler through the wild neighborhoods of Massachusetts.

Anslee's adventures are just getting started! To stay in touch and be the first to learn when *The Return of Magic: Book 2* is available, sign up for K.E. Blair's email list on her website and connect with her on her social channels.

Website: https://www.mythandmagicbookclub.com/publishing/keblair

Instagram: https://www.instagram.com/authorkeblair/

Goodreads: https://www.goodreads.com/author/show/44097734.K_E_Blair

Also by K.E. Blair

The Hidden Crown (The Return of Magic #1)
The Veiled Kingdom (The Return of Magic #2) – Coming 2024

Also by Myth and Magic Publishing

Jillian Witt

Compass Points (Compass Points #1)

Tangled Power (Compass Points #2) – Coming Spring 2024

Thank You

Thank you for reading The Hidden Crown – Anslee's adventures are just getting started! Will you take a moment to leave a review? Word of mouth plays a big role in a book's success, and other readers want to hear from you!

Review on Amazon
Review on Goodreads

9 798989 153015

Printed by Libri Plureos GmbH in Hamburg, Germany